It was time to add her secret ingredient...

How could she, though, with Chino standing not two feet away? Well, maybe she could slip it in while Penny Beth engaged in her childish pouting. Hallie sneaked a small brown bag from its hiding place, dumped it quickly into the pot and stirred. She breathed a sigh of relief, then looked up and realized with a start that Chino was watching.

"What was that you just added?" he asked.

"Buffalo chips," she said, keeping a straight face.

"Yuck. You're kidding, of course." Penny Beth covered her mouth.

Hallie shrugged. She was a fast learner.

Chino grabbed a spoon and helped himself to a taste. "Hmm," he murmured. "Interesting..."

Hallie held her breath. Would he guess correctly? Should she admit it if he did?

"I know." He snapped his fingers. "Ground mesquite blossoms!"

"Nope. Forget it, Chino. I'm not telling." Hallie crossed her arms. "Why don't you tend to your cooking and let me tend to mine?"

Dear Reader,

Nearly every weekend, somewhere in the United States, chili aficionados from all over gather for fun and earnest cooking. (Of course, each cook claims his or her chili is the world's best!)

My first introduction to official cook-offs was in the state of Washington. A professor at the college where I worked, a man known in chilidom as Tarantula Jack, sparked my interest in chili by winning the International Chili Society (ICS) World Championship Cook-off in California. He followed that win by hosting a regional cook-off on our campus. ICS cooks end up with cash prizes.

In the name of research, I followed the cook-off road to Oregon, where the Chili Appreciation Society International (CASI) was holding a state championship. I learned that organizations can sponsor sanctioned CASI cook-offs and that entry fees go to charity. But don't let that fool you—CASI competitors are as fierce as their chili is hot.

Then I moved to Texas—not just for cook-off research, but it didn't take me long to learn that Texans are *serious* about chili.

Jalapeno Sam Lewis and his charming wife, Betty, shared the "true chili story" with me. My thanks to them for providing information on cooking Behind the Store, which they swear is the site of the "first ever" cook-off—now a yearly memorial to founders Frank Tolbert and Wick Fowler. Sam informs me this group cooks to further the "romance" of chili. *Muchas gracias* to him also for wangling me a personal invitation to the granddaddy of all cook-offs held each November in Terlingua, Texas. (By the way, this isn't Sam's first book dedication. You'll find his name in James Michener's *Texas*.)

As to how all this tastes—ask my husband, Denny. He ate his way through a whole lot of chili as an official judge before *Some Like It Hotter* came to an end.

Happy reading!

Roz Denny

3520 Knickerbocker #224
San Angelo, Texas U.S.A. 76904

SOME LIKE IT HOTTER
Roz Denny

Harlequin Books

TORONTO • NEW YORK • LONDON
AMSTERDAM • PARIS • SYDNEY • HAMBURG
STOCKHOLM • ATHENS • TOKYO • MILAN
MADRID • WARSAW • BUDAPEST • AUCKLAND

ISBN 0-373-03336-2

SOME LIKE IT HOTTER

Copyright © 1994 by Rosaline Fox.

CHAPTER ONE

HALLIE BERGSTROM was glad school was nearly out for the summer before she got herself fired, instead of tenured. She didn't know what had possessed her last night, marching stodgy Mrs. Perkins, head of the Cedarville School Board, down to her homeroom to show her the misspelled graffiti splashed across the walls. She'd done it because she'd been fed up, Hallie thought as she tugged two heavy boxes of books out to her scruffy pickup.

Twice the administration had promised to paint the classrooms something other than putrid green. And twice they'd failed to keep that promise. Still, she might not have acted so rashly if each fall the field house hadn't gleamed with fresh paint and the football field been newly seeded.

Not that she disliked football. But Cedarville seemed pathetically lax about the three R's. Fathers only cared if their sons excelled in sports and mothers groomed their daughters to marry.

But shock of shocks, Mrs. Perkins had agreed with her. In today's heat, though, Hallie found that moving all her personal leather-bound volumes of the classics home so someone could paint her classroom was more punishment than triumph. It was unseasonably hot for the month of May in the Texas hill country.

Wishing for even the slightest breeze, Hallie lifted the thick fall of honey gold curls off her perspiring neck. She trudged back into her room only to discover she'd run out of newspapers to line the last few boxes. "Damn it all." She glanced around guiltily to be sure no student had overheard.

"Is English teacher in a snit again?" A pretty redhead popped around a scarred door casing, her twinkling green eyes alight with laughter.

"I'm out of packing paper, Evie." Hallie smoothed a loving hand over gold lettering cut deep into burgundy bindings. "My shed gets dusty."

The newcomer—Hallie's best friend, Evelyn Bowen—grinned. "I'll share. I'm finished packing. Guess I'm not nearly so attached to my crummy old math and physics books. I just threw those suckers in boxes and nabbed a jock to cart them out to my car." She disappeared, returning moments later with a small stack of papers. "Sorry, looks as if you're reduced to today's news."

Hallie accepted the *Cedarville Sentinel*. "Have you even read it? Otherwise, I'll wait."

"Be my guest. I doubt it's changed since yesterday. You know, I was so excited about the prospect of getting these rooms painted, I forgot to keep books out to finish the last two weeks."

"Who'll notice? No one's cracked a book in my classes for a month. I could write a thesis on excuses. Prom, sports, haying. They all come first."

Evie laughed. "Well, your rousing speech to the school board last night may shock a few parents into action. You even surprised me."

Hallie continued to separate the paper into sections, listening to Evie with half an ear. Folding open the business section, Hallie stuffed it into a box, then yanked it back out. A man's smiling face stared out at her from the top column. Her mouth went dry.

Even in grainy black and white, Chino Delgado's midnight black eyes invited sin. Those eyes, coupled with his lopsided smile, catapulted Hallie back to the year she'd arrived in Cedarville. She'd been a gauche freshman from Minnesota, painfully thin and shy. Quite different from the outspoken woman who had taken on the entire school board. But that was the year both her parents had died in a freak avalanche, and she'd been unceremoniously dumped on an aging grandmother's doorstep.

Everything rushed back—her first day at a new school, when she'd been too scared to take in the matronly secretary's warnings about steering clear of the wild Delgado boys. Four in all, the woman had cautioned—Jesse, Chino, Cody and Kirby. Names foreign to a girl growing up with boys called Bjorn and Tor. Hallie's memories tumbled into one another.

Who could have guessed she'd walk out of the office that day and run smack into Chino Delgado? She'd scrambled on her hands and knees at his feet, retrieving her scattered books while he silently undressed her with those bedroom eyes.

Chino was three years ahead of her in school—and lightyears ahead in anatomy and physiology. Yet, for whatever reason, he made educating her his pet project. She would gladly have been his conquest, but then he backed off…and the day after he graduated, married someone else.

Hallie's cheeks still burned with embarrassment. How naive she'd been that night in the hayloft, thinking he loved her. Lord help her, but even now she had difficulty considering herself lucky that he'd only let his friends *think* he'd scored. Strange how the pain of rejection outweighed good sense in even the most sensible of women.

"What is it, Hallie?" Evie responded to her friend's pensive silence.

"Did you read this?" Hallie shook the page under Evie's nose. "It's terrible what he's proposing for Cedarville."

"Who? What?" Evie looked genuinely puzzled.

"Chino Delgado. That's who." Hallie whispered his name. "According to this article, he plans to buy the Cellar and turn it into a Chilipod, or whatever he calls those places he owns. It's an outrage."

Evie grabbed the paper to hold it still. "He calls them houses. Chino's Chili Houses." She clutched one hand to her heart. "That man do ooze sex appeal." Her soft drawl spoke of a Louisiana heritage. "I ate at one in Dallas when

I attended a math conference. The food was good. What's the matter, aren't you pleased to see a homctown boy succeed?''

"Where's your loyalty?" Hallie demanded. "If he turns the Cellar into a glass-front drive-through, *where,* pray tell, will our literary group meet?"

Evie shrugged. "I didn't think of that."

"Oh, he's clever, pulling this now. In two weeks we break for summer." Hallie frowned. "Yesterday I left a schedule of our next fall and winter meeting dates with Joe Bonner. Why do you suppose he didn't mention this?"

"Ya got me."

"What are you two so het up about?" A thin, rather bookish-looking woman peered in, adjusting wire-rimmed glasses on her nose as she skirted a half-packed box of books to join them.

"Did you read this tripe about Delgado Enterprises buying the Cellar for a fast-food chain, Glynnis?" Hallie yanked the paper out of Evie's hands and placed it in those of Cedarville High's only art-and-drama teacher. Glynnis, too, was a member of Hallie's literary group, but she had an even more personal interest in the Cellar's fate. For several years, she'd been dating Joe Bonner, who owned it.

Now she appeared stunned. "Joe hasn't said a word, I swear. What about our poetry readings? I've signed up five people from Austin to hear Lowell Pippin's newest works next fall. Will we have to cancel him?"

"No kidding?" Evie blinked. "Hallie actually talked Pippin into coming here to read Stargazer's Fantasies before it's released? What a coup!"

Hallie waved the compliment aside. "Look, don't you agree that someone in Cedarville should try to prevent this . . . this blight on our community?"

Her friends first seemed hesitant, then both nodded.

Hallie snapped her fingers. "I know. Evie, you stop on your way home and have a chat with Penny Beth Frazier. This is her byline. She may know more than the article says.

And Glynnis, since you and Joe are an item, you need to go see if they've signed any kind of contract yet."

"Some item," Glynnis muttered. "He still won't make a commitment."

Hallie commiserated a moment, then said, "I'll call Delgado Enterprises. The article mentions a public-relations department in San Antonio. Meet back at my house for dinner."

"Good plan, Hallie. This may only be speculation," Glynnis offered, refolding the paper. "I can't believe Joe would sell."

Evie shook her head. "Maybe not. I heard that Chino's at the ranch. His father recently suffered a heart attack."

"I didn't know that," Hallie said. "But surely he and Serita won't leave their gorgeous hacienda in San Antonio for long. According to last month's *Cultural Upbeat*, they just finished renovations." Hallie didn't say she'd saved the pictures of Chino on his front steps with the interviewer. There'd been none of Serita, come to think of it, and no *real* information. Just facts about the restoration, the designers and so forth.

"Where have you been, Hallie? Chino's marriage to Serita hit the rocks almost before the honeymoon ended," hooted Evie. "Sweet li'l Serita is in the process of dumping hubby number three. Although she's back, too. I saw her in Bronson's cosmetics department last week—complaining about how we don't have a soul in town who does nails right."

Hallie's jaw dropped. "Third? I never knew."

Glynnis rolled her eyes. "Seems a crime, doesn't it, when here's three of us without even *one* husband."

Hallie stammered, "So wh-who's the current lady in Chino's manor?" She couldn't help asking, even though deep down she didn't want to know.

Evie shook her head. "Nobody legal, I'll lay odds. At least not if one can believe his sister-in-law. Jesse and Babs's youngest son is in my Sunday-school class. And ol' Babs does love to chatter on about the family."

"Doesn't surprise me." Glynnis snorted. "All four Delgados were into bottle blondes with big—"

"Glynnis!" Hallie sounded shocked.

"Well, it's true," Glynnis said defensively. "Sometime when you're over, remind me to show you my yearbook. Two-thirds of the girls in my graduating class bleached their hair and stuffed their bras. All in hopes of bagging Kirby."

Evie chuckled. "Same in mine. Only it was Cody. And I'll never show you my yearbook. My hair turned orange." She rolled her eyes. "We'd moved here that year from Shreveport. My mother threatened to put me in a convent if I didn't let my natural color grow out over the summer. Ask her today, and she'll still say those Delgados are spawn of the devil."

"She's right," Hallie said. "And tonight, we'll discuss ways of exorcising the Cellar of one Delgado—the Chili Baron, to be exact."

Evie and Glynnis joked about Chino's new title as they left.

LATER THAT EVENING, Evie entered the small house Hallie had inherited from her grandmother. She sniffed the air. "Mmm. Chicken smells great. But you disappoint me. I was expecting chili."

Hallie thrust a bowl of green salad toward her. "Don't mention that word until after we eat. Gives me indigestion just thinking about it."

Glynnis, loaded down with two bottles of wine, banged on the back screen. Evie set the salad on the table, let her in and watched as she plunked both bottles on the counter. "After my chat with Joe, the rat, I thought we'd want to drown our sorrows in high octane."

Hallie felt a surge of anger. "So it's not just speculation! Delgado's PR department told me zip. They were tight as clams."

Glynnis looked glum. "Joe's mother took a turn for the worse last week and he had to put her in a nursing home in Dallas. He says the Cellar isn't making money. Chino got him a job tending bar in a top Dallas night spot, then offered to buy Joe's equity."

"How convenient—the sneak." Hallie burned herself on a cob of corn. She brought the stinging finger to her mouth, which ended her dark mutterings.

Evie took down three wineglasses and began to pull the cork on the chardonnay. "Listen to this, ladies," she said, throwing all her muscle into the task. "You know how Penny Beth's hair was always kind of cow-pie brown?"

Hallie and Glynnis both looked up. "Well, today, she's champagne blond." The cork popped and the wine spilled over Evie's hand. "If you ask me, this all means Chino's up to something."

Evie poured, then all three sat staring dejectedly at the array of food.

"I suspected as much," Hallie confided. "I called a member of the town council and asked if she thought they'd consider the historical value of the Cellar before granting a building permit."

"And what did she say?" Evie prompted.

"I got the distinct impression our council's main interest is the tax revenue Chino's franchise would generate."

Glynnis helped herself to a chicken leg. "Materialistic morons. What do they care about history? Midas mania. Every last one."

"Couldn't our group meet here once a month, Hallie?" Evie suggested, glancing around the warm, neat kitchen with its homey antiques.

Hallie raised a stubborn chin. "We have something special in the Cellar. Something unique to Cedarville. People go for espresso and atmosphere as much as to hear the readings. It's more than a building."

"According to Joe," Glynnis interjected, "all we do is take up space. He claims his electric bill runs more than we spend. If I'd been brave, I'd have suggested combining our incomes." She sighed. "We'll never get married now."

Evie snapped her fingers. "Hey, Hallie. Lovesick here just gave me a brilliant flash. You're blond. Why don't you run out to the ranch and appeal to... to Chino's intellect? If you get my drift."

"Me?" Hallie's fork clattered to the floor. "I'd sooner be boiled in oil. Let someone else be your sacrificial... v-virgin," she sputtered, bending to retrieve the fallen utensil. "My forte is writing steaming letters—not steaming car windows. He can't ignore a letter."

Glynnis paused in the middle of nibbling corn. "You guys are cruel. Evie calls me lovesick and Hallie might have said sacrificial *lamb*."

Hallie rose quickly and went to rinse her fork.

Glynnis continued. "Of course I'm not blond, but I'm probably the only virgin over twenty left in the valley." Unhappily she reached for a paper towel to wipe her fingers. "Joking at a friend's expense isn't like you, Hallie."

Evie straightened, her eyes narrowing on the woman who seemed to be welded to the sink. "Hallie? It was a joke, right?"

Silence.

"Well, well," Evie murmured. "So all the rumors about the Delgados leaving nary a fair-haired virgin in Cedarville aren't true."

"Men and marriage. Is nothing else important to you two?" Hallie charged, returning to the table, her cheeks and ears glowing pink. "Let's just finish eating and I'll go write that letter."

Evie downed her wine, then stood and carried her plate to the sink. "Hallie, what's with you? It's unAmerican not to sit around with a group of women friends and complain about men and your sex life."

"I don't know," Glynnis lamented, pushing her plate away. "One cannot discuss what one does not have."

"Glynnis, honey," Evie interrupted, "in Hallie's case, at age twenty-six, one should fabricate. In yours, well, men in the hill country like women with a little padding. With the exception of Joe Bonner," she said wryly. "And now even he's leaving Cedarville."

"That's it, ladies." Hallie stood. If she'd ever wanted to discuss something—say, for instance, why Chino Delgado had told his friends he'd made love with her that night in the hayloft when he *could* have, but didn't—she was too embarrassed now to bring it up.

"Okay, we'll leave," Evie grumbled. "But I still think we should compare notes. Cripes, even airheaded Mavis Pritchard went to El Paso and came back married. My profound condolences, Hallie. I had no idea you were... well, you know... What d'you say we forget this stuff with the Cellar and go have a summer fling? According to Ginny O'Dell, the rodeo circuit is *the* place to find single men."

Glynnis shoved Evie toward the door. "She's delirious, Hallie. I keep telling her the only preferred stock at a rodeo are the Brahman bulls. You go right ahead and write your Chili Baron."

"He's not mine," Hallie was quick to say.

"No?" Evie teased. "I told Penny Beth you coined the term. Soon the whole world will know—including Chino. So you'd better sign a fictitious name to that letter, unless it's supposed to be a ploy to attract him."

"It's no ploy," Hallie asserted, trailing out behind them.

Or was it? She was to ponder Evie's suggestion every time she rushed home and eagerly scanned her mail. *No,* she decided every time. If she never saw Chino Delgado again it would be too soon. All those years ago, she'd loved him and he'd trampled that love. And he'd lied to his pals, to boot, besmirching her reputation in the process.

So why, after two weeks without so much as a whisper from the president of Delgado Enterprises, did Hallie find herself furious enough to shoot off a second blistering letter to Kirby Delgado, vice president? Because she'd heard he was brilliant and less of a womanizer? Because she thought he might respond to a concerned hometown citizen? Or... because he'd tell Chino?

No matter. Kirby didn't answer, either, and suddenly school was out. Hallie decided all the Delgados were cut from the same cloth. Such insensitivity called for stronger tactics. Afraid her literary-club members, who were mostly teachers, would scatter for the summer, she elected to call an emergency meeting and hand-delivered the notices.

Sometimes Hallie wondered why she put herself out so much for a group that never seemed to reciprocate. Except that the monthly gatherings had become her deepest passion. In Cedarville, Texas, there was little enough to be passionate about—if you aspired to something more intellectual than bull-riding or collecting firearms.

Not that she'd ever leave Cedarville, Hallie thought with a guilty start. Deep down, she'd grown to love it. At first she hadn't believed she would, even though Gram had told her time and again that Texas got into a person's blood. With all its blue sky and limitless land, it gripped people's hearts and imaginations. Their roots went deep. Visitors who came, stayed. Residents who left, for whatever reason, returned at the first opportunity. In a word, it was *home*.

She stripped off her gloves and stopped weeding Gram's prize berries. If she didn't hurry, she'd be late to the meeting. Tardiness was a trait she didn't like in others—and one she worked diligently to overcome in herself. Hadn't Gram claimed all hopeless daydreamers were consistently behind?

Hallie shook off the thought, showered quickly and scanned her closet for something cool to wear. After much vacillation she settled on a pink and white sleeveless dress Gram had given her for her last birthday. A dress she'd never worn because the old woman had passed away soon after. The dress held sad memories. But perhaps she should stop letting memories rule her life. Gram would be pleased to know she'd be wearing it tonight as spokeswoman.

On her way into town, Hallie actually managed to laugh. Cool frills and a hot issue. Both would have appealed to her grandmother. But how would the rest of the scholarly group receive a speech designed to incite them to riot? Well, if not exactly to *riot*, at least to get them interested in protecting the Cellar.

Judging by the cars lining both sides of the street, it was a better than average turnout. Of course, they didn't have the place exclusively. Not that she resented sharing the room with dart players. But some of them did, although it was rare now for a reader to be heckled, unless Joe was sponsoring a dart tournament including out-of-towners. With all these cars, she wondered if he was.

Forced to park in the next block, Hallie practically ran back to get there on time. If she'd had more presence of mind, she might have asked Evie to read the opening speech she'd written espousing the quality of life, traditional values and local heritage. People tended to follow Evie like sheep. Maybe it still wasn't too late, Hallie thought, tripping on the last step.

A motorcycle type in black leather, walking in behind her, kept her from falling headfirst through the double doors.

"Thanks." Hallie tossed a vague smile over her shoulder, her mind racing ahead toward picket lines and sit-ins. Her apology for being late froze on her lips.

Lounging on a bar stool facing her—and *lounging* was the most civilized term Hallie could think of for the shameless way he sat, pant creases pulled tight over his lean hips—was the numero-uno subject of tonight's meeting. Chino Delgado.

The man wearing black leather almost ran her over. And as if it wasn't unnerving enough for Hallie to find the enemy seated in her camp, she'd swear the man behind her patted her rear before he sidled past. What should have been a resounding rebuke sounded more like a squeak. Flustered, she could only march past the bar, pretending every stool was empty.

To regain her composure, Hallie stopped and ordered her usual café mocha. It was then she realized that newly blond Penny Beth Frazier was draped all over Chino. Hallie's jaw ached as she ground her back teeth.

Chino Delgado wasn't quite sure what had gone on between Hallie Bergstrom and the low rider, who had by now joined a group of dart players in a noisy alcove off to his right. At first he thought they were together. That shot his well-rehearsed greeting all to hell—although he did realize he simply wasn't as prepared to see her as he'd thought. By the time she stuck her pretty little nose in the air and swept past, he'd completely lost the advantage of surprise.

Penny Beth's endless chatter drifted in one ear and out the other. Chino toyed with the elaborate band on his summer Stetson until he became aware of his nervous fidgeting and stopped. After all these years he still felt guilty about letting his high school buddies assume he'd made out with Hallie in that hayloft when he hadn't. But back then he'd been young and wild, and he'd had an image to uphold. She evoked soft, unmanly feelings in him—feelings that even now made the hair rise on the back of his neck.

No more than four feet from Chino, Hallie waited impatiently for her coffee. Why didn't he say something? Had he forgotten her? She simmered. He'd know her next time for sure, the way his fathomless dark eyes, ringed by long sooty lashes, kept raking over her. He hadn't changed one iota, Hallie thought, feeling his gaze reverse the order and travel from her toes to her head.

"What did you do, Joe?" she muttered when he delivered her drink piled high with double-whipped cream. "Turn the air off in here?"

Always quiet and soft-spoken, Joe Bonner glanced around at the wall vents, each with a narrow red flag blowing furiously. He shrugged. "Nope. Shall I dump this and fix you something iced, instead?"

"No. I'll drink it." Hallie gathered the folder holding her speech. She took a sip, heedless of the whipped cream that coated her upper lip.

Abruptly Chino faced the bar. Wiping a damp palm down one pant leg, he reminded himself sharply that he was no longer nineteen and hot-blooded. But neither was the woman holding the whipped coffee still sixteen and innocent. Why, then, was he annoyed to see that Hallie Bergstrom had matured so...so favorably? Absently he traced designs in the condensation on his longneck beer and studied her with renewed ferocity.

Hallie suffered through a second insulting inspection. An inspection that hit her like a hot blast from a furnace. It had always been one of Chino's favorite tricks—undressing her with his eyes—especially once he found it sent her skittering like a mouse for a hole. Well, she wasn't a mouse now, and it was high time she took charge and showed him.

She tried to catch Evie's eye.

Her friend glanced up and immediately joined her. "For heaven's sake, did you invite him?" Evie hissed.

"Coincidence," Hallie said, balancing the hot cup on her folder.

Evie's brows rose. "Is it also coincidence that he's got the press in his corner?"

Hallie was loath to admit she found that part disappointing. "So what?" she said. "We have the right to assemble. The question is how best to get the club to back us." As they discussed a plan, in Hallie's acute peripheral vision—the "eyes in the back of her head" every high school teacher cultivated—she noticed Chino disconnect himself from the bar stool. In that limber way of his he moseyed toward them. Hallie's heart beat frantically. By the time he reached the center of the room there wasn't a nerve in her body that wasn't screaming for deliverance.

Panicked, she looked for an avenue of escape. The best she could manage on short notice was to grab Evie's arm and plunk both of them down at a table for two.

All too soon, Chino hovered over them—handmade cowboy boots, snow-white Stetson and all. Ignoring Penny Beth, who followed, he swept off his hat and shook back a tumbled disarray of black curls. Smooth as any magician, Chino helped himself to a chair from the next table and insinuated it neatly between Hallie and Evie.

"Hal?" He hesitated only briefly. "By golly. It *is* Hal Bergstrom, isn't it?" he asked, covering her ice-cold hand with a warm palm, fully aware that the masculine nickname used to irritate hell out of her. "Long time no see, kid," he rasped softly when she remained mute. "Been what? Six years if it's a day, right?" But that, too, was calculated. Chino knew to the hour how long it had been since he'd left her untouched in that hayloft.

Hallie had forgotten how fast he could get her hackles up by calling her that hateful nickname. She would just pretend not to recognize him. "Ten years," she blurted, long before the decision to ignore him was transmitted to her brain.

Something deep in his dark eyes flared in satisfaction, and Hallie yanked her hand away. Damn, but she'd fallen into another of his traps. It took several seconds to remind herself that she'd grown up—even if she hadn't outgrown loving him. "I'm fine, Chino," she managed to say evenly, as if she hadn't already played into his hands. "I've been teaching English at Cedarville High for a few years."

"I heard," he murmured.

"Then no doubt you also heard I'm immune to innuendo and flattery." But for some reason—maybe because he still wore the subtle after-shave that drove her crazy—her cool slipped. "Tell me," she demanded tightly, "does your presence here mean you've had second thoughts about inflicting one of your tasteless culinary hybrids on our town?"

A nerve jumped in Chino's jaw.

"Does she mean Chili House?" Penny Beth asked from behind him. She placed a manicured hand on his arm, clucking sympathetically.

Hallie watched him shrug it off and actually found herself feeling sorry for the reporter. "Maybe you didn't get my letter." She took another sip of her mocha drink and measured the crowd who strained to hear.

Unobtrusively Glynnis glided over to align herself with her friends.

"Oh, I got both missives, teach." Chino's statement was just loud enough to reclaim him the floor.

Penny Beth dragged out a notebook and pen.

"Any part you didn't understand?" Hallie asked sweetly. "Words you need defined, perhaps?"

Chino leaned to within a millimeter of her chin. With a forefinger, he scooped off a smidgen of whipped cream that clung tenaciously to a corner of her mouth. Soft as a whisper, he trailed the still-moist drop across her lower lip. "After I left Cedarville, Hal, I did dual majors at Texas A&M."

Lifting his finger, Chino tasted what cream remained. "I graduated summa cum laude in agriculture and marketing." He smiled.

Blood raced through Hallie's veins like an overdue freight train. A tiny gasp slipped through her parted lips.

Evie coughed. Glynnis made ineffectual noises in her throat.

Chino tilted back on two chair legs and balanced there. "Six years at Texas Christian, Hal, and it appears all you learned was how to emasculate a man in writing. What a waste of—" he paused, studying her mouth "—raw talent." His hooded gaze slid up to lock with hers. "Oh, I understood every word," he said in tone that implied, *hell hath no fury like a woman scorned.*

Hallie wanted to deny everything—to say this wasn't about the two of them, it was about the Cellar. Heat climbed to her cheeks as he let the chair drop back into place, rose gracefully and pushed it back under its rightful table.

She couldn't let him humiliate her again. Grabbing her notes, she marched to the front of the room. "You want to destroy Cedarville's primary landmark!" she accused him, finding it easier to breathe with the width of the room between them. "Is everyone here aware that the brick in this building was actually bought for the governor's mansion in Austin?"

There were a few nods. "It's unclear why it ended up in Cedarville, but the mayor's wife claimed it for a hotel she had dreamed of building. One night someone stole the whole load. And right under the sheriff's nose, Joe Bonner's grandfather and his friends built this saloon." Hallie turned to Joe, but saw impassivity there. She flipped a page. "The mayor's wife is said to have hired men to blow up the saloon. Not only did they fail, but the Cellar was so solidly built it was the only structure left standing after the tornado of 1939 leveled the entire town. Imagine that, will you?''

Hallie pointed at Chino. ''It wasn't until '42 that Chino's father claimed the grazing lands south of town and built his ranch.'' She walked down an aisle and spread her palms eloquently. ''I beg you,'' she implored, ''can we, in good conscience, let a Johnny-come-lately turn such a legendary building into a sleazy Tex-Mex fast-food...eatery?''

Chino crossed his arms and stared at her for a moment. Suddenly he threw back his head and laughed.

Penny Beth wrote furiously.

Hallie heard a ripple of responding laughter sweep through the crowd. Whatever had made her think she could best him? Chino Delgado always could charm the spots off a leopard. He'd reduced her arguments to insignificance.

Rubbing his jaw, Chino asked, ''Have you ever eaten at one of my restaurants, Hal?''

Hallie grimaced. In all honesty she hadn't, and she shook her head.

''Tell you what.'' He dug in his coat pocket and produced a fistful of coupons. ''I happen to think Delgado chili is sort of a legend, too. My grandfather attended the first-ever official Texas chili cook-off. Dad's pushed to have the Bowl O' Red named the Texas state dish. As a family, we support an organized movement to have Congress declare chili con carne America's official food.'' Tossing his hat onto a table, he grinned. ''I'll go so far as to guarantee that Chino's Chili House offers a dish for every taste. Why, half my menu's old family recipes—every one a cook-off winner.''

Starting with Hallie, he moved among the tables passing out certificates for free dinners. She saw they were good at any of his thirty restaurants in Texas and New Mexico. *Thirty.* She hadn't dreamed he owned so many. No wonder he could gobble up the Cellar.

"Hey, Chino," a loud male voice goaded from the darker alcove, "is it true everyone in your family's won that cook-off down in Terlingua 'cept you?" The question was accompanied by a round of good-natured guffaws.

Chino didn't laugh.

Evie leapt suddenly to her feet. "Is that the truth?" Shading her eyes, she peered into the smoky perimeter of the room, seeking confirmation.

"What's the real skinny, Chino?" yelled a wizened man at the bar.

"I haven't won yet." Chino's reluctance to admit as much wasn't hard to read. "But this year I've got a new secret ingredient." He finished passing out coupons and donned his hat as if to leave.

Evie caught his sleeve. "What's so tough about making great chili? Hallie makes the best I've ever tasted." She threw him a cagey smile. "I bet she'd share her recipe—if you promised to leave the Cellar alone."

Chino glared at her. "You haven't got a clue, lady. Do you think some amateur can just enter a cook-off and win?"

He made the statement with the "You don't know what the hell you're talking about" smirk Hallie remembered so well.

Glynnis jumped to her friend's defense. "But what if Hallie entered your old cook-off—and did win?"

"Glynnis, no!" Hallie objected.

Chino's dark eyes glittered for a moment, then he laughed. "Well, now. The first cook-off is next week in Buzzard Flats. Tolbert's rules. *If* over the summer she picks up enough points to cook in Terlingua, and *if* by some remote chance she wins..." A corner of his mouth quirked upward. "*If*—and *only if*—that happens, I'll gladly scrap my plans for this building."

"Oh, wow!" Penny Beth exclaimed. "Can I print that?"

"My word is my bond," he said smoothly, as if daring anyone to refute it. Without so much as another glance at Hallie, he stalked off—in that infuriating hip-rolling swagger that was practically a trademark of the Delgados.

Still writing, Penny Beth scurried off behind him.

As Chino passed the dart players, some whistled and stamped their feet. Except for the sullen man who'd first heckled Chino, they all pledged him their support.

Evie and Glynnis raised their arms, smacked palms and whooped. Taking up the challenge, they began to chant, *Hallie, Hallie, Hallie.*

Her jaw went slack. Groaning, she closed her eyes. Where in heaven was Buzzard Flats? And what were Tolbert's rules? Dazed, she gathered her scattered notes. The thoughts that came spontaneously to mind had to do with virgin sacrifices. Considering who she was up against, Hallie feared she might lose more in this venture than a historic building and some dumb, macho, chili cook-off.

CHAPTER TWO

HALLIE SAT in her kitchen impatiently waiting for the first pot of morning coffee to finish perking. Her restlessness increased as she read the front-page article in the *Cedarville Sentinel* concerning last night's debacle. Damn, but Penny Beth Frazier did have a way with words.

Of course, Penny Beth's article was rather one-sided—in Chino's favor. But then, the reporter didn't know that after Chino had left the literary-club members toasted Hallie and made her out to be some kind of avenging heroine. A person could really get caught up in adulation. Hallie sighed. She could hardly refuse to represent them. Not after the whole bunch stayed for second cups of espresso, and everyone lauded her courage and wished her luck in saving the Cellar.

But the article didn't make it sound as if she was defending the building. On the contrary, it sounded as if she'd had the gall to challenge a favorite son. As Hallie reread Penny Beth's clever words, she began to realize the bottom line in this whole deal. She'd been the victim of a railroad job, pure and simple. A victim of the fastest, slickest B & O treatment this town had ever witnessed. Courtesy of her best friends, too.

She hadn't slept well and felt only marginally better about the chili challenge for having gotten up before dawn to look up the whereabouts of Buzzard Flats. It wasn't featured in *Backroads of Texas* as she'd first feared. On the state map it looked close to the interstate. Which didn't mean it was any great shakes as a town, but at least it was listed.

A knock rattled her back door just as Hallie's coffeepot emitted its last gurgle. "Come in," she called, reaching for two cups rather than one. She smiled. Glynnis, no doubt, taking a detour on her morning run—feeling guilty about her part in last night's fiasco.

Maybe she'd make her beg for coffee, Hallie thought, picking up the pot.

A louder knock. Hallie filled both cups and smiled. Glynnis must really feel bad; the door wasn't locked. Hallie had been out at first light to feed the birds. "It's open," she called, closing her eyes to savor the aroma of fresh-ground "vanilla bean." Gourmet coffee was a treat she only indulged in when school let out and she had time to sit and enjoy it.

The door creaked open, and Hallie laughed. "Wise of you to test the waters, Glynnis Kelly. A white flag might do the trick. If we weren't such good friends, you'd be buying your coffee at the local Stop and Go."

A deep masculine chuckle had Hallie whirling, slopping coffee on the counter over the rims of two ironstone mugs. A startled cry lodged in her throat. All she could think was that she stood barefoot in her most disreputable nightshirt, with her hair in a right-off-the-pillow frizz. While Chino stood framed in her doorway, fully clothed in canvas duck and leather, direct from the pages of *Old West Outfitters*.

"Get out," she barked when at last she found her voice.

Chino couldn't have moved a muscle to save his life just then. He stood there, galvanized, as he watched the play of sunlight in her shoulder-length hair. Mellow gold, the color of fine Puerto Rican rum splashed over crystal ice. He needed that coffee. His mouth felt drier than sagebrush.

"Out, out, out!" Hallie's voice rose. "Now, before I count to three."

"Yep. You sound like a teacher, all right." Chino collected his equilibrium enough to toss a battered, flat-crowned hat on top of the paper she'd been reading. Helping himself to a seat, he grumbled, "Trouble is, Hal, I never met a teacher who had a strategy once she got past three.

Coffee smells funny," he observed, sniffing. "What'd you do, burn it?"

Hallie wished for something to throw. She grabbed up the mugs, then realized hot coffee was dripping on her bare feet. She all but slammed both cups on the table. "This is fresh-ground, you imbecile. I did not burn it." In the heat of anger she had forgotten how thin the cotton of her sleep shirt was. Until Chino's gaze shifted.

Choking back belated fury, she ran from the room and returned only after she was covered neck to ankle in her heaviest chenille robe. She didn't care that it was too hot to wear this time of year. What she cared about was staying hidden from those disturbing eyes. So she'd wear it until Chino tired of playing cat-and-mouse and left her alone.

But he sat calmly sipping her vanilla coffee and scanning the list of upcoming bull sales. Her own coffee cooled in the cup.

Figures, she thought, glaring down on his tangled thatch of dark curls. "To what do I owe this unexpected visit?" she asked warily, snatching her mug and retreating behind the center island. Gram's kitchen table was just too small to accommodate the both of them.

"Why don't you ease up? You act like I'm Jack the Ripper."

"It's before breakfast, Chino. And I'm a teacher. I have a reputation to maintain. People do gossip, you know."

He leaned back, looking amused. "That worries you at twenty-five?"

"Twenty-six," she snapped. "You have three minutes before I call Chief Potts."

"Ouch. You play hardball now, Hal. I don't remember you being so tough."

"If you're notching your belt, you can take credit for that."

He frowned and looked away.

"You've wasted two minutes," she warned, gathering the robe close beneath her chin. She hadn't meant to let him know that she was still bothered by what had happened back then. Yet she'd all but spelled it out—Chino Delgado had rejected poor little Hallie Bergstrom and now she wanted him to pay. Hallie dumped her coffee and poured fresh. "This isn't about the past," she said, knowing that wasn't entirely true. He would be forever linked to her past.

"Okay." He held up a palm. "I came to apologize for the way I let things get out of hand last night. Hank Edwards is the loudmouth who started everything. He's bent out of shape because Jesse beat him three years ago at Terlingua, and last year Kirby did the same. Hank's bragged all over Texas that he's going to beat the socks off me this year."

"What's that got to do with me?" she asked.

"Come on. I know you can't possibly make a chili that'll place. I'll get Penny Beth to write something face-saving for both of us. No sense in you shelling out money for entrance fees, membership dues and the gas it takes to get to cook-offs."

"And the Cellar? What happens to it?"

"What do you mean, what happens to it?" he asked sharply. "I bought it fair and square. I intend to open a Chili House in Cedarville. What else?"

"What else, indeed?" Hallie's eyes narrowed on what she judged to be his phony self-effacing smile. "Forget the maligned little-boy routine, Chino. You think I don't know male angst when I see it?"

"Excuse me?"

Hallie set her cup down carefully and slapped both hands down on the counter. "Sorry. My mistake. I assumed summa cum laude graduates in dual majors understood three-dollar words. Let me break it down for you, Chino. It's very simple, really. You'll be in deep horse puckey in your chili kingdom if my recipe turns out to be better than yours."

"I'll what?" He came flying out of the chair. "You can't honestly think—" With a jerky motion, he picked up his hat and jammed it on his head, then stalked toward the door, still sputtering.

"Pride goeth before a great fall, Delgado. See you in Buzzard Flats."

His dark eyes spit fire. Then, with lips pressed in a tight line, he touched the brim of his hat, withdrew and slammed her back door so hard it rattled the small glass panes in the upper half.

It was only after Hallie heard the screen shiver with equally loud reverberations and a vehicle spit gravel in the driveway that she released her pent-up breath. She immediately bent to the task of digging out Gram's chili recipe.

An hour later, she gazed lovingly at the well-used card written in Gram's precise hand. The recipe was old, but—she frowned at the thought—maybe it wasn't all that great. Some small part of Hallie wondered why she hadn't allowed Chino to get her out of this mess. But then, Gram always did maintain that Hallie was too stubborn for her own good. 'Course, on the other hand, one of Gram's favorite philosophies had been: if a body has a hill to climb, waiting won't make it any smaller. And from where Hallie sat, she faced a mountain of her own making. Well, maybe not exactly of her own making. She had two good friends who shared the blame. Funny, how conspicuously absent they were today. Normally one or both would have stopped by for coffee.

She called Evie first. Getting no answer, she tried Glynnis. Her answering machine was on. Half an hour later when her phone rang, Hallie rushed to pick it up, certain it was one of her friends. She was wrong. It was the first of a series of crank calls that ruined her morning. Several men and a few women called to ask what Hallie thought she was doing, making light of a Texas tradition like the Bowl O' Red. At least, that was the gist of the nicer calls. There were also a number of strongly worded suggestions that she should back off and let Chino win. Was this all his doing?

It made her mad, having her privacy invaded like this. But it hurt, too. Cedarville wasn't so large that some of those folks calling didn't know her. And Gram. Everyone had known and loved Gram.

She tried again without success to reach her friends. Darn, but she could use a word of encouragement about now. Good grief, people were talking chili cook-off here. Not the Olympics!

When noon came and went, and neither Evie nor Glynnis had had the decency to show their faces, Hallie climbed into her truck and did what she usually did when she was out of sorts. She drove up to Kerrville to the library. The trip through the rolling hills offered glorious countryside and a perfect opportunity to let her mind drift and her anger unwind. Plus, she needed to read up on this so-called Texas tradition.

At the library, Hallie found more than she wanted to know about chili cook-offs—starting with the first big challenge in 1967 up to today's Chili Wars. Nowhere did she find any list of Tolbert's rules, although the man's name was mentioned several times, along with a Mr. Fowler. She checked out several books that claimed to be authorities on the subject. If she was going to go up against that no-good louse, Hallie decided she'd better learn everything possible.

She poked around town considering what she'd learned. She visited a new craft store and her favorite boutique, then treated herself to a chocolate ice-cream cone before heading home. And she felt better—until she turned down her drive and discovered Chino Delgado sitting on her back porch.

Hallie got out of the pickup, but left her library books on the seat. She'd be darned if she'd let him catch her doing research!

"Now what do you want?" she asked ungraciously.

He unfolded himself from the steps. "I brought you an application form and the *Goat Gap Gazette*. It's kind of a newspaper for serious chili-heads. It lists the places and dates of cook-offs. Gives point standings and that sort of thing."

Hallie shifted her purse to the other arm and stretched out a hand to accept the papers. "Thanks," she mumbled, supposing a chili-head was what one aspired to be in this gastronomic phenomenon.

Chino removed his hat and slapped it against his thigh.

"Was there anything else?" she asked, brow furrowed.

"Ah." He kicked at a loose rock, then jumped when it clanged against her hubcap and ricocheted back. Annoyed, he growled, "You do know Texas chili doesn't have beans, don't you?"

Hallie crossed her arms. "I *have* lived here ten years. And excuse me, but I thought I didn't have a prayer of winning. Why are you telling me all this?"

"Because I don't want you to go and make a fool of yourself, that's why." He put his hat back on and yanked it low over his eyes. "Adding beans to chili at one of our cook-offs is tantamount to sacrilege."

"I don't know what's motivating you, Chino, but I don't think you have one altruistic bone in your body. I appreciate the application, but perhaps you should save your touching concern for someone who doesn't know you as well as I do. Furthermore, tell your fan club to quit phoning me." She stormed up the steps and into her house. Inside, she leaned against the door, her legs shaking, until she heard his Jeep rev and roar out of the drive. "Damn, damn, damn." Why couldn't he just leave her alone? He had, for ten years.

After going back out and retrieving her books, she listened to the messages on her answering machine. One was a lengthy discourse from a rough-sounding man who called himself Big Daddy. He ended his diatribe by saying he made the best chili in Texas and was gonna "whup her butt" and Chino's, too, at Buzzard Flats.

"Whew!" Hallie sank into a chair. Maybe she'd take Chino up on his offer to get her out of this, after all. To heck with saving face. She started to erase everything left on the machine, thinking it was just more of the same. But then, concerned that the remaining messages might be from Evie and Glynnis, she backed it up. Another gruff voice rumbled, "Ms. Bergstrom? This is Ram Delgado. I'm in room

410 at Our Lady of Guadeloupe hospital. Come see me to-day."

Hallie ran the tape to the end and erased the whole thing. "Like father, like son," she sneered, half under her breath. She'd never even met Romiro Delgado. Who did he think he was, ordering her around? She could see why everyone called him Ram. He was well-known as a stubborn old man who always expected to get his own way.

Hallie poured a glass of milk, and as she searched for chocolate chip cookies, she thought about how difficult it must be for a man like that to be confined to bed. Any time she'd ever seen him, he was loading or unloading heavy things from a truck. He was probably six inches shorter than any of his sons, but more robust. Handsome, with just a touch of silver at his temples.

Hallie gave up her search for the cookies and drank her milk. What could it hurt to humor him? As she recalled, he had kind, dark eyes and a nice smile that belied his reputation—and that of his four hell-raising sons. Maybe this would be an opportunity to find out more about those chili-contest rules, too. A man in the hospital would have his defenses down, after all, and just might be willing to talk.

The hospital was on a knoll, nestled in a stand of live oaks that overlooked the Guadalupe River. Hallie thought that if a man had to be confined anywhere, this might be more acceptable than some places. The stucco buildings were well cared for and the grounds immaculate. Inside, the floors gleamed and the wood trim was rubbed to a high patina. No antiseptic smell, at least not on the fourth floor where the rooms seemed more like private suites. Hallie supposed money bought this type of luxury. She stopped outside a door with the number 410 etched on decorative tiles.

Even as she hesitated, the door opened and a pretty, petite woman with short-cropped hair the color of summer wheat sped out the door. She was nodding and still talking to someone inside. She almost ran into Hallie as the door closed behind her. "Oh," the woman exclaimed with a little laugh, "you startled me." Then her eyes made a quick sweep, taking in Hallie's casual clothes. "Sorry," she said, her smile receding, "only hospital personnel and family are allowed in this room."

Hallie rechecked her note. "This is Mr. Delgado's room?"

The pretty woman nodded. "And you are?" she demanded bluntly.

Hallie thrust out her hand and gave her name. "Mr. Delgado's expecting me," she declared, assuming that was true.

"Ah, yes." The blonde's eyes sparkled. "You're the thorn in Chino's side." The dimpled smile returned. "I'm Cody's wife, Ivy. Do you live in Cedarville? I don't think we've had the pleasure of meeting."

Hallie checked out the younger woman's designer attire, then glanced down at her own jeans, washed enough times to show the mileage. She shrugged and murmured that she was too busy to spend much time in town.

"Well, I'm not a local," the other woman said amiably. "I'm from California. Cody and I met at Stanford, in law school. He got homesick for the ranch and left before the bar exam. I took it there, then I came to see what was so great about Texas." She grinned. "As you can see, I'm still here. Goodness, I'm blabbering. Bad habit for a lawyer. Go on in, Hallie." Her blue eyes sparkled. "Just don't let him intimidate you."

"I'm not even sure what he wants," Hallie said. "But since you called me a thorn in Chino's side, I suppose it must be regarding the chili thing."

The woman nodded. "I've only been in the family a year, but already I've learned to respect chili." She winked and patted Hallie's hand. "Gotta run," she said. "I promised Babs I'd baby-sit. Good luck." She turned and jogged toward the elevator.

Hallie felt as though she'd met up with a steam roller. Ivy Delgado was a bundle of energy. A lawyer, she mused. Glynnis would be surprised to hear that, after the way she'd described the Delgado women. Taking a deep breath, Hallie rapped solidly on the door.

"Come in, come in," a loud voice boomed.

Hallie didn't think the Delgado patriarch sounded much like a sick man. She opened the door a few inches and peeked inside. The bed was empty. She stood for a moment, letting her eyes adjust to the bright sunlight streaming in through tall windows.

"Come in or stay out," the voice thundered again, "I don't have any patience for nurses playing peekaboo." A dark-haired man in a wine red silk robe rose from a chair near the windows and beckoned her in.

Hallie entered and shut the door. "If you're always this short-tempered, Mr. Delgado, I can't think you'll be out of here very soon."

The man looked startled for a moment, then sank into the chair again. Laughing, he motioned her closer.

His laughter sounded just like Chino's had the other night, Hallie realized. A swift pang tightened her throat.

"Who are you?" he asked. "You're not in uniform, so you aren't after my blood. I heard you talking to Ivy, so it's too much to hope you'd be here for anything nefarious." He enjoyed his own joke immensely.

"That depends on your definition of nefarious," she said. "I'm Hallie Bergstrom. The way you sounded on my answering machine, I'm quite sure you expected me to have two heads and horns."

He studied her for a moment. "Your chili any good, girl?"

Hallie dropped her purse on the bed. "It's very good, Mr. Delgado. And I'm a woman."

He made a steeple of his fingers. "Damned if you ain't. Did Chino tell you how much you look like his mother? My deceased wife?"

Hallie faltered for the first time. Her knees buckled, and she sat in the chair opposite him. "N-no," she stuttered. "We knew each other in high school. He never even hinted as much."

"Curious," the elder Delgado said. "Well, I shouldn't have mentioned it. Now I suppose you'll find some way to use it against him in this chili battle you two got going."

"I don't fight dirty, Mr. Delgado. If I win, I win fair."

The man tugged at his ear and stared at her for a long moment. "Well, then," he said, "how about a game of chess? Every damn one of my boys cheats. If you play me, maybe I can win for a change."

She glanced at the board, which was ready for play. It was a beautiful set. Jade and ivory. Looked antique. And probably cost a mint. "If they cheat, sir, perhaps they learned from you. It takes two to make an honest game."

"Damn it, girl—uh, Hallie. Now you even *sound* like my Rebecca." He slanted her a wide smile as he pulled the small table between them. "I like you, gal. Sit a spell. We'll see how much you know about chess."

It was Hallie's turn to grin. "And chili?" she teased.

He shook his head. "Maybe yes. Maybe no."

They'd been playing chess and chatting about inconsequential things—some chili, some not—for about two hours when the door suddenly flew open, and Chino charged across the room. Confronting his father, he bellowed, "Ivy told me you were consorting with the enemy. But I didn't believe her."

The elder Delgado reached his right hand to the left side of his chest, as if reaching for a cigarette. On not finding either a pocket or a pack of cigarettes in his robe, he looked exasperated and turned that exasperation on his son. "If I was consorting, it wouldn't be any business of yours. But you can damn well bet the lady would be closer to my age— and my door would be locked. Now, apologize to Miss Bergstrom—on your way out."

Chino's mouth opened and closed. A dull red stain moved up his neck. "I meant fraternize. Not. Not..." The red splotch spread. He turned to Hallie, something unreadable in his eyes.

Never having seen him at a loss for words, Hallie enjoyed every minute. Casually she picked up her elegant ivory queen and boxed Mr. Delgado's jade king into a corner. "Checkmate," she said, her gaze meeting Chino's before sliding to his father.

Chino looked from Hallie to the board to his father. With suppressed rage, he spun on his low-heeled Ropers and left the room as quickly as he'd entered it.

"Well!" exclaimed Hallie's partner. "That boy distracted me. This game wasn't fair. I demand a rematch."

Hallie started to protest, but soon threw up her hands and shook her head. "You're really something, Mr. Delgado. I suspect I know exactly where your sons learned to cheat. I honestly don't have time for another game today. How about if we call it a draw and I come back another time?"

"Promise?" he demanded, eager as a child.

"I promise. Right now I have to go home and read up on chili. Next time I come, I'll know what you're talking about when you use terms like high torque, capsicum and Chilympiad. And I'll still beat you at chess."

"Horsefeathers," he said. "Torque is how they measure the heat from peppers. Capsicum is the chile—the pepper itself, spelled with an *e* on the end. Chilympiad is the men-only cook-off. It's held once a year. More cooks compete there than anywhere else. And I intend to practice chess all week while you're boning up."

"You won't tire yourself out, will you?" she said, picking up her purse, then turning to look at him, her eyes filled with concern.

His darker eyes softened. "I'll be good as gold. Got me a goal now. I intend being there to root for both you and Chino in Terlingua."

"Both?" She started to say that was silly, but something in his expression stopped her. She couldn't say for sure, but she thought maybe he wasn't seeing *her* just then; he was seeing the woman he'd lost a long time ago. The woman he said she reminded him of. She slipped out quietly, leaving him to his memories.

She didn't expect Chino to be waiting in the parking lot. But he was. And he was not a happy man.

"Just what in hell are you trying to prove, playing footsie with a man old enough to be your father?" he demanded, blocking her access to her truck.

"You're despicable, and your father was right. You do owe me an apology."

"What were you doing up there?"

"Playing chess." She brushed past him and yanked open the door of her pickup. "Not, as you so vulgarly suggest, footsie."

"You expect me to believe you took time out to be a candy striper?"

She looked at him as she might a bug under a microscope. "I have no control over what people think, Chino. I learned that lesson a long time ago. Now I'm going to drive out of this parking lot. If you don't step aside, you may be sharing a room with your father."

He kept one hand on the truck's side mirror until she released the emergency brake, hit the ignition, and her vehicle started to move. Then he let go and jumped aside.

Hallie drove to the end of the lot before she looked back. He was still watching. That unnerved her. She decided she wouldn't come back to play chess with Chino's father unless he guaranteed his son wouldn't show up. These encounters brought back too many memories. Too many feelings she'd thought long buried. If she wasn't careful, she might repeat an old mistake. Hallie vowed then and there that she'd be hanged before she let Chino Delgado humiliate her again.

Evening shadows had settled, bringing a rare cooling breeze. When she got home, Hallie opened both doors, enjoying the sound of crickets as she ate her solitary meal. She still hadn't been able to raise either of her friends and was feeling just a little blue. After dinner, she relaxed in the living room with the books she'd checked out of the library.

All at once someone hammered on her front door. Chino again? For a moment, Hallie's heart accelerated. Then she heard Evie and Glynnis arguing, and one of them called her name.

Suddenly Hallie didn't know how she felt about seeing them, since they'd obviously avoided her all day. So she let her heart settle and took her own sweet time about un-hooking the screen.

A long, slender arm appeared out of the dark. On the outstretched palm rested a half-gallon of Häagen-Dazs chocolate-chocolate-chip ice cream. A second arm appeared waving a can of dark-chocolate syrup.

"Idiots," Hallie burst out. "Where have you been all day?"

"Would you believe digging up the inside poop on chili cook-offs?" Evie said, forcing her way inside past Hallie.

"Yeah," Glynnis agreed, trooping in behind her. "After we read Penny Beth's article, we got worried."

Evie threw an arm around Hallie's shoulders. "You've got to believe me, Hallie. I had no idea what a monster I created. The controversy over who makes the best chili ranks right up there with who was right in the Civil War. I'm sorry, good buddy. I truly am."

"Surely it can't be all that bad," Hallie ventured.

"Believe me," Evie interrupted, "you don't know the half of it. Häagen-Dazs doesn't make enough chocolate ice cream for *this* binge."

Glynnis looped an arm through Hallie's and turned her toward the kitchen. "I rousted Joe out of bed at the crack of dawn and asked him for the names of locals who might know about these cook-offs. Other than the Delgados, that is." She helped herself to three of Hallie's cereal bowls. Evie began scooping heaping portions of ice cream into them.

"Enough." Hallie grabbed her hand.

"I don't think so." Evie fixed gloomy eyes on her friend.

Glynnis plopped a spoon into each bowl and poured on the sauce. "The first dude we went to see had more hair than I do and was built like a Sherman tank. He said anybody who knows beans about chili knows chili has no beans. Then he all but threw us off his property."

"Yeah, nice guy," Evie said, pulling out a chair and digging into her rich dessert. "So then we went to see this old duffer," she said around a mouthful. "He claimed his chili was an ulcer scorcher. Best chili in Texas, or so he said."

Glynnis screwed up her face. "Yuck, Evie. Do we have to tell her what he said he used for meat?"

Evie nodded. "Maintained he started with wild boar, then tossed in a little rattlesnake for flavor. He seemed nice, but I decided he was a nut-case. Except he did send us to Luckenbach. That's where they have the ladies' competition every year."

Hallie stopped with a spoon halfway to her mouth. "You two have been all the way to Luckenbach today?"

"That's what we've been trying to tell you," Glynnis said. "Evie had no idea she was opening up a can of worms. Those folks in chilidom are dead serious. We think you should back out now, Hallie."

Hallie looked from one to the other. "You heard Chino. His word is his bond."

"So?" Evie said.

"So, what about mine? Anyway, you got me into this."

Evie winced. "I said I was sorry."

Glynnis carefully separated out a large chocolate chip and pushed it aside to save for last, as she always did. "Uh, Hallie . . . we thought maybe the three of us could sit down with Chino and explain how it happened, in the heat of the moment and all that. Don't you think he'll understand?"

Hallie set her bowl aside. She'd hardly made a dent, even though it was her favorite flavor. She thought about Chino's latest insinuations. Suddenly it seemed very important to compete with him on a level other than the personal. Compete—and win. "*You* don't understand. *We* are in this to save the Cellar. And I'm not backing out."

Evie reached for Hallie's bowl. "I was afraid you'd say that. Do you mind if I finish this off? I predict it's gonna be a long hot summer."

Hallie handed it over.

"Thanks," Evie muttered. "Maybe I'll go into a chocolate coma and sleep until Christmas. Hallie, I gotta tell you square. Today we heard names like Badass Chili, Lightnin'

Bolt Chili and Hellfire Chili. And you're going to enter one called Gram's Chili? Come on! You'll be crucified.''

Hallie gave Evie the look she saved for football jocks who handed in papers written by their girlfriends. "It's not the name that wins, Evie. It's the taste. Aren't you forgetting you announced to the world that Gram's Chili is the best you'd ever eaten?''

CHAPTER THREE

BUZZARD FLATS was not the end of the earth. But it certainly looked like it could be. Hallie, Evie and Glynnis sat in Hallie's pickup on a dust-covered rise and surveyed the chili cook-off site in silence. They'd been on the road since six-thirty. It was now eleven, check-in time for contestants, and already it looked as if every available shade tree had been staked out by some other cooking team.

"Will you look at that," Evie said at last. "They have trailers with canopies, motor homes with awnings *and* all the shade. What do we have?"

"A folding table and a pickup truck," Glynnis supplied.

"Well, now," Hallie said brightly, "maybe the trees aren't all taken. You two sound like the voices of gloom and doom."

"I wonder why," Glynnis said dryly. "We stayed up half the night packing, left before the roosters crowed, and if you saw a motel in the last fifty miles, I don't know where."

"Maybe they're beyond where we turned off, Glynnis. Goodness, the map shows five or six towns along this section of the interstate."

"Yeah," Evie grumbled, "and judging by the ones we already passed, I doubt there's a total population of ninety among the lot."

"Do you want to leave? Shall we go home and just let Delgado have the Cellar?"

"No," Evie and Glynnis muttered, although neither with much conviction.

"Then let's go down there and set up. We'll ask around about motels. Today's the barbecue competition. We cook chili tomorrow."

"Didn't you say there was a dance tonight?" Evie lifted her sunglasses. With some disenchantment, she scanned the area.

"It listed one in the flyer." Hallie let out the clutch and drove on down the bumpy road to the encampment. If anyone was peeved, she thought, it should be her. She didn't have one suitable thing to wear. Wanting to look cool and professional in front of Chino and his buddies, she'd packed two split skirts with blouses and a white dress for the dance. White—when dust rolled in waves from beneath her truck.

Hallie stopped in one such reddish cloud outside the only permanent structure in sight and grimaced. "Do you suppose it'll settle soon?"

"Wait and see," Evie said doubtfully.

Through the gritty haze, Hallie saw Chino Delgado step out of one of the larger motor homes and start toward them. He was wearing a red-and-white-striped shirt, red suspenders, black jeans and polished black boots that nearly reached his knees. Did the man have stock in a boot company? she wondered savagely, considering her inappropriate soft-leather flats.

Darn, but she'd been hoping they wouldn't run into him until after she had everything well in hand. Had he been watching for her? Very likely. No doubt he planned to start gloating early.

Reluctantly she rolled down her window and waited.

"Hi," he greeted them with a smile. "Sorry I didn't think to mention that you need to get here early. Hop down. I'll get you something cold to drink, then we can walk around. Maybe there'll be a spot left with shade."

Evie clambered out of the passenger side. "I hate to be indelicate, Chino, but before I drink anything more I need to use the facilities."

"Amen," Glynnis seconded, slower to descend.

Chino pointed out a building with a flat roof, almost hidden in a thick copse of trees. "How about you, Hallie? A cold soda or a pit stop?"

"I'll take a rain check on both. I'd like to locate a place first."

"No problem. We'll meander that way, ladies." He pointed. "Help yourselves to whatever's in my fridge. Join us whenever."

"Tomorrow?" Evie joked. "I'd like a nap."

Chino chuckled, took Hallie's arm and steered her along a narrow path between a row of motor homes.

"Even a sliver of shade would be nice," she told him. "I didn't bring a tarp."

"But you have a tent, right?"

Hallie licked her lips, not meeting his probing gaze.

"No tent?" His eyebrows shot up. "Where in the devil do you plan on sleeping?"

"In town." Glynnis spoke from behind them. Apparently she'd decided to take a shortcut through the vehicles. "How far would you guess to the nearest motel, Chino?"

"A hundred miles. Give or take five." His gaze seared Hallie.

"Miles?" Hallie gasped. "One hundred miles?" She turned to face him and a gust of wind caught her skirt, lifting it above her knees. Blushing, she tried to get a grip on the fabric, but failed. By then, Glynnis had gone on, shaking her head and complaining to herself.

A gray-haired man with a full beard and a hefty paunch was lighting a blackened barbecue near where they stood. "Yo, Chili Man," he called, after loosing a wolf whistle. "Some classy lassie. She yours?"

Chino tugged at his ear and flushed. Hallie found that amusing.

"Naw," Chino denied. "The lady's new to cook-offs, Dutch. I'm just showing her the ropes."

Well, he was certainly quick to set that straight.

A plump woman, with wise but faded blue eyes, stepped from the small trailer behind Dutch. "She the little gal who claims her chili's gonna best yours in Terlingua, Chili Man?''

"Where'd you get that notion, Mama Claire?" Chino asked, a shade too glib to suit Hallie.

The woman laughed and her whole body shook. "Challenge like that travels damn fast through the grapevine. Reminded us old-timers of the dispute that started all this hullabaloo." She winked at Hallie. "If I had any money, it'd be on you, gal. Us women gotta stick together. Took long enough for these loudmouthed men to finally let us cook. Last bastion of the good ol' boys, you know?"

Chino nudged the back of his Stetson, tilting it forward over his eyes. "I can't believe you heard this nonsense all the way over in Tyler. That no-good Habanero Hank started it. Whole thing's out of hand, if you ask me."

"Like it or not, Chili Man," the old fellow behind the barbecue advised, "you and the Classy Lassie got a battle goin' to the finish." He tipped a flat-brimmed hat banded with fat plastic chili peppers at Hallie. "May the best man win." Then the old guy ducked fast. Chubby as he was, he managed an agile escape when the woman, Claire, took after him with a skillet.

Hallie presumed it was all in fun, although she might not have known it from Chino's scowl. "Look," she said, spreading her hands, "let's end this right now. Promise you won't renovate the Cellar."

He cupped her chin with a suntanned hand, forcing her to look up. "This battle goes beyond the Cellar. And it goes beyond winning in Terlingua. This started long ago."

"Stop it, Chino." Hallie pulled from his grasp. "I don't know what you mean." She ran ahead a few yards, before halting beneath a lace-leafed tree. Her hands curled into fists. Every nerve tensed.

He caught up to her and grabbed her arm. "I'm not finished saying my piece. According to Jesse, Dad—for whatever reason—is dead set on watching us duke this out. I don't like it, but it's the first thing to spark his interest since he had that last attack. Even if your chili's lousy, we'll see it through for him. Understand?''

Evie wandered back just then. She carried a soft drink, cadged, no doubt, from Chino's supply. "Chino, what's with all the funny names I've been hearing?" She seemed unaware of interrupting a heated discussion. "Some dude over there called you Chili Man. Introduced himself as Hannibal the Animal and his buddy as Red-Eye Rex." She rolled her eyes.

Chino stepped away from Hallie. "It's part of the hype. You can cook with a guy for years and never know his last name or what he does for a living. Doctors, lawyers and politicians rub elbows with John Q. Public at these things. Occasionally you'll meet somebody in their other life, but generally all you know is the name they use here. I have a higher profile because of being in the chili business."

Glynnis returned before the conversation ended. She nudged Hallie. "I kind of like Classy Lassie, don't you? I heard someone call you that. I think I'll whip off a glitzy banner for you when we get home. I see a lot of the trailers have them."

Evie struck a pose. "Wouldn't Sophisticated Lady be better? I was thinking of those neat backdrops your class painted for the senior prom, Glynnis. You remember, PUT-TIN' ON THE RITZ in silver glitter."

"Wait." Hallie put her hands on her hips. "Don't go making this a theater production or a three-ring circus."

"Yeah," Chino growled. "Don't waste money on trappings yet. Terlingua is where we get into showmanship, and it sounds to me as if Hallie may be thinking of backing out."

"Why would I?" she demanded. "It only takes nine points to qualify for the finals. If anyone packs it in, it'll be you."

"If I recall," he snapped, "you don't have very thick skin. Some of the fellows can get kind of rowdy at competitions. Especially in Terlingua."

Hallie's brows dipped. "Are you insinuating I'm a wimp, Delgado?"

"I'm telling you, sometimes things get down and dirty. Look at you in your Bo-Peep skirt and ballet slippers. This isn't a Betty Crocker bake-off."

Hallie's hands were balled and her shoulders squared before he finished talking. "I wasn't aware there was a dress code. Next time I'll look like a trail driver. Now if that spot over there isn't taken, I believe I'll set up shop." She stomped off toward a skinny mesquite tree.

"Fine." He yelled after her. "Toss me your keys and I'll go bring your truck down."

"Thank you very much, but I'm quite capable of doing that myself."

"Boy," Evie said in a low tone, "you sure do know how to ruffle her feathers, Chino. At school she has a reputation for being even-tempered."

"You mean mad all the time?" came his terse reply.

Glynnis shook her head. "Just the opposite."

"You two have some kind of history?" Evie queried.

"Like how?" Chino stuck out his chin, thumbs under his suspenders.

"I think Evie means like a lover's spat way back when or something," Glynnis volunteered. "We both moved to Cedarville after you graduated. Seems to me I remember a vague rumor about you and Hallie. She was a junior when I was a freshman the year I moved from Cleveland." Glynnis sucked in a deep breath. "Hallie sensed how I felt being an outsider. She went out of her way to be nice. So I only half listened to the rumors. Darn, I can't remember."

Chino pulled his suspenders out a few inches and let them snap back. "Don't study too hard on it. You know how gossip is. Now if I can help y'all with anything, just yell." With that, he left.

Evie watched him thread his way between the puffs of smoke billowing from barbecue cookers. "There's something between those two."

Glynnis wrinkled her nose. "Well, if Hallie wants us to know, I imagine she'll tell us. Look at all this dirt, will you?" She squinted to avoid the rooster tail of dust Hallie kicked up as she tramped up the incline. "Jiminy Cricket, Evie. I'm sorry I vetoed the rodeo."

"I'm with you," Evie returned. "Do you suppose we could both plead sick tomorrow and stay in the motel?"

"That's assuming we find one." Glynnis wrinkled her nose as she watched Hallie jockey her truck to a stop and leap out in a whirlwind of dust.

All three coughed and were sweating profusely by the time they finished setting up the table. But they kept at it until they'd unloaded the small gas stove and all Hallie's cast-iron pots and pans.

"We better take the cooler with us, don't you think?" Hallie asked. "To refill it. That ice has to last until I need the meat."

"You think it's safe leaving stuff here?" Glynnis muttered, watching a moose of a man pull up at the next campsite. He seemed to be eyeing them with dislike. He made little pretense about wanting their meager shade.

Hallie didn't budge. "I'll ask Mama Claire to keep an eye on things. I think she likes me. Now that I see what people do, we'll bring Gram's tent-trailer next time. It's one of those lightweight soft-sides with a cooler on top. I didn't know everyone camped out."

Evie fanned herself with a paper plate. "Where's the next one? Someplace more civilized, I hope."

"Fort Worth."

"Hey, that's nice." Glynnis perked right up. "Hotels, motels and five-star nightclubs."

Hallie walked away. "The newsletter said it's near the stockyards."

"Oh, great," Evie groaned. "Steeped in the aroma of the west."

"Will you look at that." Glynnis jabbed Evie sharply in the ribs and pointed to a motor home that had just rolled in. It was as big as a house.

"Penny Beth Frazier," Evie exclaimed when the door opened and the reporter stepped out. "Jeez, wouldn't you know. What do you suppose she's doing here?'' They watched the woman in skintight jeans get out and stretch.

"It's a free country," Hallie observed on her return. "Hey, maybe she'd sublet us a space on her floor tonight."

"She probably has other plans. For you know who, doing you know what." Evie waggled her brows. "Surprise, surprise, they're directing her into a slot right next to Chino."

"Is sex all you think about, Evie?" Hallie asked, annoyed. "She writes for the newspaper. They probably want a follow-up on her first story."

"Sure," Evie agreed, "and I have a bridge I'll sell you, Hallie."

Hallie ignored her. "I asked Mama Claire to keep an eye out. We'd better go if you want to get back for the dance."

Fifty miles down the road was a wide spot aptly named Dead Man's Junction. There was a general store of sorts and, fortunately, cabins. Hallie booked one. Still, every mile of their drive back to the cook-off, Evie and Glynnis griped.

"So it had a cockroach in the shower," Hallie said. "The owner was nice about getting it out. He explained they haven't rented it in a while."

Glynnis made a face. "This rust color on my skin isn't instant tan, you know. It came out of the shower pipe."

"I had no idea 'air-cooled' meant the place only possessed one broken fan," Evie interjected. "And for that price..."

"One night," Hallie reminded. "We'll be there one night, and the sheets were clean. I checked."

"Good," Glynnis muttered. "This dance better be worth the suffering is all I've got to say. Holy cow!" she exclaimed, breaking off. "The place has been invaded since we left. Tent city."

"Complete with Christmas lights for the dance. Mmm, smell that barbecue," Hallie murmured. "I, for one, am ravenous."

"Do you think it's safe to eat here? Some of those pots don't look like they've been washed in years." By now the three friends were walking toward the lights, and Evie's voice carried.

Several tough-looking characters stepped into their path, asking if she didn't know that the only good contest utensil was a well-seasoned one. Properly chastised, Evie fell silent. Hallie figured it for a first.

Mama Claire spied them and motioned them over. "Where've you been, ladies? You missed the barbecue judging. I took second place. Beat Dutch out altogether." She laughed gleefully. "He's off somewhere sulking. Anyone wanna taste? Grab a plate."

Hallie turned to survey her friends and ran smack into Chino. He, too, had changed; he now wore hip-hugging jeans and a bright blue shirt with a colorful silk kerchief tied loosely at the open neck. His flashy blue boots matched the feathered band ringing his Silver Belly hat. Penny Beth Frazier clung possessively to his left arm, but for the life of her, Hallie couldn't have said what she was wearing.

"Did you find a place to sleep tonight?" Chino asked, encompassing all three in his generous smile.

"A palace," Hallie said smartly, just as Evie blurted out, "A roach-infested rat hole in a place called Dead Man's Junction."

He looked amused. "Slight difference of opinion. Would someone care to elaborate?"

Hallie helped herself to a plate and began piling it high with Mama Claire's barbecued beef. "Beauty is in the eye of the beholder," she quipped.

Taking the hint, Evie clammed up.

"I wish I'd thought of it earlier," Chino said. "You could have bunked at my place, and I'd have thrown a sleeping bag in the back of your truck. It's going to be a great night for sleeping out."

"No need for that." Penny Beth giggled. "I have loads of room."

"Nice of you to offer," Chino said, deliberately misunderstanding. "Of course they'd be more comfortable in your rig."

Penny Beth blinked, then she opened and closed her mouth several times like a fish looking for bait.

Mama Claire looked on with indulgence. "Chili Man, you always got more honeybees flittin' around you than a honey pot." She winked and nudged Hallie. "Ain't that so, Lassie?"

"Don't ask me," Hallie countered. Before she could add that she didn't flit, and if she did, she'd be a whole lot more choosy about where she flitted, she took a healthy swallow of Mama Claire's barbecued beef. For one terrible moment she imagined she was on fire. She choked repeatedly and her eyes watered.

Chino disconnected himself from Penny Beth and slapped Hallie on the back. "Claire, you've been using habanera pepper sauce again, haven't you? Get her a glass of milk. That stuff'll blister her palate."

Grinning, the older woman disappeared into her small trailer and came back with a tall glass of ice-cold milk. "I forget it's an acquired taste."

Hallie drank it down without drawing a breath. "You took second place?" she croaked, wiping her eyes. "Do the judges have asbestos teeth?"

Chino chuckled. "We refer to this as baptism by fire. You'll learn to carry a fire extinguisher when you taste-test." Whatever else he might have said was cut off by the band striking up. The others wandered off, following the sound. Chino stayed behind and asked softly, "Sure you're okay?"

Hallie nodded. She edged away to dump the plate of food into a trash receptacle. "I wasn't expecting it, that's all. Not from her."

"Lesson number one. Don't trust anybody at a cook-off. A newcomer is fair game for these kinds of practical jokes."

"I'll remember that," she said, gingerly running a finger over her lips.

His eyes followed the path of her fingertip. Almost without thinking, he reached out and tilted her face toward the light. "Your lips don't look blistered. You do have a milk mustache, though," he told her, his voice dropping to a husky whisper. For a moment they stood close together, his hands lightly exploring her arms. Then, the next thing he knew, he was kissing her.

She should have seen it coming, except that her defenses were down and the initial touch of his lips was as soft as eiderdown blowing in the wind. A kiss all the same—like the ones she remembered, only better. Once Hallie realized what was happening, Chino was already pulling back, surprise creasing his brow. And didn't she just know what came after that expression! Rejection. Rather than wait to suffer humiliation again, she turned and fled.

He might have called out for her to stop, or he might have given chase. She had the advantage of darkness and a head start to give him the slip. Avoiding the dance, she walked— or stumbled—in the dark until she was afraid of getting lost or snake-bit. Carefully picking her way back, Hallie slipped into her truck and tried to prepare herself to face him in tomorrow's competition. Not a simple task after that kiss.

She was tapping a finger on the dash, thinking how easily he'd ensnared her again, when all at once the door jerked open and she almost tumbled out.

"Where in hell have you been?" Chino's fingers curled around her narrow shoulders. "Do you know I've been hunting you for three damn hours?"

"Two," she declared, straining to check her watch.

He rolled his eyes. "Two. Three. Who cares? I had half the camp searching."

"Why?"

"Why?" He made a strangled sound, and his fingers tightened on her flesh.

"Yes, why?" She laughed—purely a nervous reaction. "You sound like a parrot, Chino."

"I was worried," he admitted, sliding both hands down her arms. Lifting one of her hands, he carried it to his lips. His dark eyes were filled with something akin to pain.

"Don't." She pulled away. "We're opponents. Nothing more." She cleared her throat. "I see Evie and Glynnis coming. We have a fair distance to travel back to our motel. If they're finished dancing, we'll leave."

"Look, if you're mad about the kiss, I apologize. I was out of line. Stay here tonight. Sleep at my place. I don't want you driving those roads in the dark."

"You *were* out of line," she agreed. "Let's leave it at that."

They were still skirting one another warily when Hallie's two friends came to stand beside Chino.

"You found her," Evie said. "I told you she hates parties."

Glynnis took in her friend's white face. "You sick, Hallie?"

"No. But I'm ready to leave."

The two women glanced from Hallie to Chino. Without further ado, they took their places in the truck.

As Hallie shut her door, she glanced in the rearview mirror and saw Penny Beth run up and throw her arms around Chino's neck. With a pang, she wondered if they'd soon be doing more. But, no—she wouldn't think about that.

She saw Chino staring at the truck, then slip one arm around the reporter's waist. Coolly, he turned her toward the glitter of the dance.

Hallie's heart tripped over itself on its way to her toes. She knew Evie and Glynnis expected her to comment. Deliberately, she turned the radio on full bore and drove in silence all the way to the cabin. There, she set the alarm, told them what time to be ready in the morning and donned her stretched-out nightshirt. Then she climbed into bed.

Next day before the sun broke over the horizon, the trio of sleepy women were again at the cook site, where quite a few teams were already up and about.

Hallie couldn't help noticing that Chino's motor home was still dark, as was Penny Beth's coach. A stabbing pain lodged behind her eyes. Refusing to think about the possibilities Evie had mentioned yesterday, she jumped out of the truck and struggled with a heavy ice chest. All at once she was relieved of its weight. More than half expecting Chino,

Hallie was dismayed to be receiving help from the moose next door.

"Women," he growled, slapping it down on the ground behind her table. "Give yourselves hernias tryin' to prove you're better than a man." He turned and spat a thin stream of tobacco juice about five feet away. Without another word, he stalked back to his own site.

"Uh, thanks," Hallie called belatedly. For a moment she considered setting him straight—not better but surely equal, she wanted to say. But what Evie muttered next distracted her.

"If that joker's a doctor or a lawyer, I'll eat Chino's Stetson. That guy's biceps are bigger than my thighs. What do you imagine his face looks like under all that brush?"

Hallie lightly scolded her friend. "He's probably very nice. After all, you thought he'd steal our stuff, but it's still here."

Glynnis murmured, "Last night at the dance I overheard a group talking. They said he wins regularly, but that he brags about using a slug of chewing tobacco in his chili. They called him Loco Lobo. Crazy wolf."

"It's hype, Glynnis." Hallie chided. "You heard Chino. Everyone claims secret ingredients. Look around. See all the brown paper sacks?"

Her two friends followed her finger.

"I don't think you can win without a secret ingredient. It's part of the mystique."

"And do you have one, Hal?" Chino's deep voice had the three whirling about.

Hallie tossed her head, discreetly trying to see beyond him to which of the units was lighted—his or Penny Beth's. Both were. That didn't tell her anything. She felt a kick of disappointment. "As a matter of fact, I do have a secret ingredient."

"You do?" Chino seemed surprised. "I'm pretty good at sorting out tastes. I'll be over later to sample your chili."

"Is that allowed?" Hallie asked.

He laughed. "Sure. A lot of us taste-test. Half the fun is seeing if you can stump the old masters. It's not like anyone's doing rocket research here."

"Are you forgetting the Cellar?"

His smile faded. "Don't you mean the hayloft?"

Hallie's color drained. He was too cruel. But that was how Chino beat out the opposition. He lulled them into serenity, then went for the jugular. She pressed her lips tight, turned and started assembling her ingredients.

Chino hooked his thumbs in his back pockets and stormed off.

"Hayloft? What's he talking about, Hallie?" Glynnis prodded.

"I haven't the vaguest idea," Hallie lied. "Are we going to stand around shooting the breeze all day or are we going to cook chili?"

Evie arched a brow. "You're the boss, but I say it's too hot to cook."

What Evie termed hot at dawn would seem cool by comparison later on. Hallie's camp stove radiated heat as her pots began to bubble. By noon, when the sun was directly overhead and there was no shade, tempers had worn thin.

"We're out of soda," Glynnis complained. "How much longer?"

Hallie wiped the sweat from her brow with her shirtsleeve. She felt the sting and knew her face and arms were beginning to burn. "Judging's at four o'clock," she said for about the fiftieth time. "Why don't you and Evie take my truck back to Dead Man's Junction to fill the chest with ice, and more soda?"

Evie pulled her shirttails out and tied them beneath her breasts. "It must be about two hundred degrees in my jeans. It's your fault, Hallie. Buzzard Flats. Dead Man's Junction. The names alone should have told you."

Hallie sighed. She wasn't going to fight. For one thing, she didn't have the energy. For another, she wanted them to go to Fort Worth with her in two weeks. "I'll pay for the sodas," she offered.

"Deal," said Evie. "Fork it over. And I'm going to see if they have any kind of hats—on your bill, too."

Hallie watched the pair leave. Sighing again, she turned the burner down another notch and stirred the meat up from the bottom. Gram swore one of the secrets to having good chili was cooking it slow. Hallie didn't know if she could stand up under this heat for several more hours of slow cooking—and she didn't mean just the chili. She closed her eyes and borrowed Evie's method of fanning herself with a paper plate.

"You're going to have sunstroke if you don't get out of this," Chino said at her elbow.

Hallie jumped and swayed.

He put out a hand to steady her. She flinched. "I want you to come sit in the shade. I've asked Dutch to help move your table under my awning."

She shook her head.

"Don't let pride make you foolish." His rebuke was gentle.

Had he shown anything but concern, had he sounded arrogant or demanding, she would have refused. But there was no censure in his eyes or his voice. And he was right. "Thank you, Chino," she said, meeting his gaze. "I'll be better prepared in Fort Worth."

A small smile twitched at his lips. "I know you will." He motioned with his hand. As if by magic, Dutch materialized and lifted her table. Soon, her chili was bubbling away in the shade, and she was sipping from a tall glass of ice water. Chino thanked his helper, disappeared inside for a moment and came back carrying a tube of medicated cream. "Aloe vera," he said, placing it in her free hand. "You look like a ready-to-eat lobster."

"I've got news for you. I feel like one, too." Setting her water aside, she smoothed on the cooling green gel.

"Don't forget your ears," he reminded in a strained voice as he turned away to check his chili.

Hallie paused, frowning at his back. Tension was back, thick in the air. She finished covering her burned skin, capped the tube and laid it on his table. "I owe you," she said simply.

"Out here we don't keep score."

Penny Beth stepped out of her motor home and joined them before Hallie could respond. "What's this?" she asked. "Enemies joining forces?" She cuddled up to Chino, looking for all the world as if she'd just showered and freshened her makeup.

In contrast, Hallie's arms sizzled, her face felt tight, and she could swear her skin had a greenish cast from the aloe vera.

Chino shook his head. "Do us all a favor, Penelope. Quit badgering Hallie and me. Write about Hank. He's determined to win, by hook or by crook. And speaking of ol' Habanero, go pester him about his new ingredient." Smiling, he set her aside.

Hallie remembered a time the Delgado smile would have wilted her knees. Now she was immune. Let *Penelope* do his bidding. Darn, it was time to add her own secret ingredient. Where were Glynnis and Evie? They should be here to create a diversion. Maybe she could slip it in while Penny Beth engaged in her childish pouting. Hallie sneaked a small brown bag from its hiding place, dumped it in the pot and quickly stirred. She breathed a sigh of relief, then looked up and realized with a guilty start that Chino was watching.

"What was that you just added?" he asked, interest lighting his eyes.

"Buffalo chips," she said, keeping a straight face.

"Yuck. You're kidding, of course." Penny Beth covered her mouth.

Hallie shrugged. She was a fast learner.

Chino grabbed a spoon, reached across the table and helped himself to a taste. "Hmm," he murmured. "Interesting. Sweet. No, make that tart."

Hallie held her breath. Would he be able to guess correctly? Should she admit it if he did?

"Pungent." Chino licked the spoon and put it down. "Did you braise your meat in wine?"

"Nope." Hallie crossed her arms. "Forget it, Chino. I'm not telling."

"I'll get it sooner or later," he said, looking smug. "I know." He snapped his fingers. "Ground mesquite blossoms. I remember tasting it once in some chili made by an old-timer—a friend of my father's."

"No." She began to fidget. "Look. Evie and Glynnis are back. Why don't you just tend to your cooking and let me tend to mine?"

"Come on," he wheedled. "Be a sport. I'll tell you what I use if you do the same."

"Sure," Hallie said dryly. She smiled as her friends trudged in and Chino jumped to help with the cooler. "And Evie will sell you a bridge."

"Moved up to the high-rent district, I see," Evie joked. She stopped and fanned herself. "Can't say I'm sorry. Is this crapshoot about over?"

"You're back in time to take my sample up to the judges. It'll be about half an hour. Remember, you promised to protect this with your life."

Evie crossed her heart.

As the minute hand climbed toward four, Chino stirred his own pot and tossed off random guesses about what Hallie's secret spice might be.

Her smile widened. He was so sure it was a spice.

At last they heard the call for the first round of judging. Evie and Glynnis filled the large prenumbered cup and took off. Penny Beth volunteered to be Chino's runner. Old hand that he was, he kicked back in a camp chair and twisted the cap off a cold beer. "Want one?" he asked.

"No, thanks." Hallie turned down the heat on her stove and paced.

Chino tugged on one ear, admiring the swish of her split skirt. "It's rare to place the first time out." He kept his tone solicitous.

She shot him a sidelong glance. "You almost sound as if you care."

"Will you withdraw altogether if you don't place to-day?"

She laughed. "And watch you start tearing up the Cellar? Dream on."

There was a commotion near Dutch's trailer, and they both glanced up. "You survived the first cut, Hallie," Glynnis announced, breathless.

"So did you, Chino." Penny Beth patted her curls and preened.

He stood and set his beer aside. "The second-round judges won't be so easy to impress. They've tasted gallons of chili."

"Are you saying my chili won't go the last mile?" Hallie accused.

"I'm saying if that was dried tomatoes you chucked in, these judges will discount your entry."

Hallie really did wish she had something to throw at him. Instead, she ignored him, turned off her stove and followed the two women to the makeshift stage crowded with cooks awaiting the final word. Hallie lost sight of Chino in the throng. When the announcement came, she was truly shocked. Hank took first. Classy Lassie second. A rotund man they called Hot Lips Hugo came in third. Evie, Glynnis and Mama Claire whooped so loud Hallie almost missed hearing that Chili Man garnered fourth. Which meant she'd chalked up three points to Chino's one. For a moment, she felt badly for him. After all, it was *his* tradition. He had brothers and a rascally father expecting him to win, to say nothing of people in the trade.

Hallie was so concerned about Chino's feelings that she missed noticing another cook—one who seemed less than pleased by her good fortune.

The exodus from Buzzard Flats began at once. Even Chino had closed down by the time Hallie had accepted her certificate. She saw him pulling out. If that didn't draw the battle lines clearly, she didn't know what did. She'd expected at least some recognition from him.

Hallie worked quietly, stowing her outfit. Evie and Glynnis were so exuberant they didn't notice that she wasn't. When they passed Penny Beth's motor home on the trip back, Evie reached across Hallie and tooted the horn. "Poor Penny Beth, she wants Hallie's secret ingredient so bad she can taste it." Evie chuckled.

"What?" Hallie broke her silence, turning in surprise. "Why?"

"Why do you think?" Glynnis prompted. "To give to Chino. He probably asked her to worm it out of us."

As they laughed, Hallie's disappointment in him shot up a few more degrees.

CHAPTER FOUR

THE MOMENT HALLIE MADE the turn into her long driveway she saw the bouquet of carnations propping open her
screen door. Her heart skipped a joyful beat. Chino had
decided to congratulate her, after all. How like him. Back
in high school, when he was trying to charm her, he occasionally slipped a rose into her locker. She'd postured as all
kids do and insinuated it meant nothing. She'd even told
him roses were pretentious to a girl who liked violets. Secretly she loved his attentiveness. And him.

Tired as she was from a new experience and the long drive
home, *any* type of flower would renew her flagging energy—and her faith in Chino.

Hallie elected to unpack in the morning. She was anx-
ious to read what he'd written on the card she saw protrud-
ing from a plastic stick. She'd soak in the tub tonight and
enjoy the sweet scent of carnations. If it wasn't too late
when she finished, she'd call and thank him.

She was glad Evie and Glynnis weren't here to see the silly
grin she knew must stretch from ear to ear as she hugged the
large vase and juggled things so she could languish in the
scent as she unlocked her back door. Why was it she
couldn't seem to control these roller-coaster feelings when
it came to a man she had every reason to dislike?

Her fingers trembled ever so slightly as she tried to remove the small card from the envelope with her name written in a very bold, very masculine hand. Her fingers shook
harder. All at once the card let loose with a sudden slurp,
and she almost dropped the vase. "So you can cook chili,"
it read. "Mi excusa." Hallie knew from her college Spanish

that meant "My apologies." She clutched the card tight and let her heart level out before reading on. "There's still chess," the note proclaimed in a broad scrawl. It was signed, "Ram."

Not Chino, but his father. Hallie's elation plummeted. What was wrong with her? She should still be happy. It was a nice gesture. He was a nice man. And lonely. It was just... Hallie sighed, leaving the vase on the kitchen counter. Weighted steps carried her down the hall to her bedroom. It was just what? a little voice nagged in her ear.

"Nothing," she answered it aloud. "Just nothing." She kicked off her shoes and stripped where she stood, opting for a quick shower rather than a bath.

It was plain that Chino had his nose out of joint because Gram's chili had beaten his the first time out. And yet she recognized there were other factors. He must have a substantial investment in the Cellar and probably envisioned it going down the drain. He'd never said in so many words that he had any interest in her aside from beating her in Terlingua—so he could turn the Cellar into a Chili House. One kiss. No big deal to a man like Chino.

And where did that leave her? Her best defense—maybe her only defense—was Gram's secret ingredient. According to Evie, he already had people trying to find out what it was. People like Penny Beth. That showed his true colors.

Hallie stood under the shower and let hot water seep into her pores. She knew from past experience how persuasive Chino could be. Especially when it came to women. Now she was glad she hadn't told Evie or Glynnis what Gram's secret was. Not that she thought he could work his wiles on either of them, but why take chances?

Wrenching off the faucets, she stepped out, dried herself, threw on a comfortable nightshirt and went to bed. Her telephone rang, but when she answered no one was there. Wrong number, she thought and went back to thinking about Chino. Let him try to worm it out of her. She plumped her pillow vigorously. He'd learn she wasn't the pushover she'd been at sixteen. Let him try his buddy-buddy rot. Not to mention his sneaky, suave kisses. Starting tomorrow, she'd be on the lookout for all his devious tricks.

Starting tomorrow. Tonight what harm could there possibly be in fantasizing a tiny bit about his devastating kisses?

Hallie found out what the harm was—a sleepless night. Reliving that darned kiss was the sole reason she was up before sunrise, scrubbing pots and washing the dirt of Buzzard Flats off her truck. Well, not the *sole* reason, perhaps. There was also the memory—the very precise memory—of how good Chino had looked. And several more phone calls with no one speaking at the other end. Wrong numbers, she hoped. Maybe just some drunk.

It was still early when Hallie called Ram Delgado to thank him for his bouquet. She found herself smoothly manipulated into visiting him that afternoon for a game of chess.

"Darn," she grumbled, tugging at the strapless halter top that matched her red shorts as she headed for the garden. There were a lot of the son's wily ways in the father, or vice versa. She thought about that as she reclaimed her tomatoes, beans and peas from the dandelions and thistles that had sprouted from thin air in the two days she'd been gone.

The sun beat down. Images of a tall, cool glass of mint tea were floating before her eyes when Hallie was jerked from her reverie by a deep cough. Believing herself alone, she stiffened and whirled around, then nearly dropped her hoe.

Chino was hanging over her back gate, a strange look on his face as he clutched the life out of a small nosegay of violets.

"Are you all right?" Hallie asked. In her concern for his welfare, she'd briefly forgotten that he was capable of all manner of tricks to gain sympathy. Raising her sunglasses, she waited for him to speak, her heart pounding.

Chino couldn't honestly say he was all right. He'd heard the scratch-scratch of her hoe and expected to find her in the garden, but he wasn't at all prepared to see so *much* of her. So much exposed flesh. Even as he gazed at her in appreciation, he saw her start to frown. "I...ah...those are the healthiest damn pole beans I've ever seen," he blurted. "What's your secret?"

Secret? Hallie suddenly recalled that she stood less than ten feet from her secret chili ingredient. Row upon row of it. She didn't dare let him into her garden—which was exactly where he was headed. "Wait!" she yelled. "Don't come another step." Hallie ran toward him brandishing the hoe. "I just fertilized. You'll ruin your new boots."

He looked at his old Ropers, then spared a glance for the dry, cracked earth that hadn't seen fertilizer in years. Any comeback he had got tangled up with breathing as she joined him. Being this close to Hallie's long, golden legs created a fine sheen of sweat on Chino's brow.

She sensed he was at a disadvantage, and although she didn't fully understand why, she found it exhilarating. "You look like a man close to heatstroke, Chino. Come up to the house. I know what you need." Linking her arm with his, she smiled and urged him forward.

He shifted the violets and stared at the rise and fall of her firm breasts, barely sheathed beneath the fire-engine red halter. "Yeah. You bet." He ran a damp palm down his thigh. "What do I need?"

"Ice mint tea," Hallie said, leaving him at the door. "It's in the fridge. Help yourself. I'm going to go pull on some sweats."

It took a moment before Chino admitted to himself that tea, mint or otherwise, was the last thing on his mind. "Score one for Hallie," he murmured around a laugh that tapered off the moment he turned to put the violets on the counter and came face-to-face with a large florist's bouquet.

At once thoughtful, Chino changed his mind about cooling off. He rummaged in the cupboards and filled two glasses. Hearing her footsteps in the hall, he braced himself. No way would he mention the carnations.

She hadn't even cleared the doorway when he pointed to the vase and demanded, "Who's the boyfriend?"

Hallie accepted the tea he offered and, after taking a sip, picked up the sad cluster of violets. "These need water."

He was still staring at the carnations.

"Are these mine?" she asked, sniffing the light fragrance.

He craned his neck, trying to read the card she'd shoved beneath the tall vase. "I, uh... Didn't you say once that you liked violets? I felt bad about not congratulating you Sunday. But I had two appointments with vendors in Dallas. It's not good practice to stand them up."

She filled a delicate white vase with water, then arranged the violets with care. So he *did* remember her preference. "Did your vendors and the family razz you?" she asked casually.

He fingered one of the pink carnations in the large vase. "Jesse lectured. Cody started to, but Ivy lit into him good. You knew? How?"

"The carnations are from your father, Chino."

"Dad?" He jumped away from them as if he'd been shot. Then his eyes turned flinty. "I hope you aren't expecting me to call you Mom."

"Very funny, Chino. I figure it's more likely that *you* asked your father to send them in order to soften me up—to find out my secret ingredient."

He smiled. "I prefer to do my own softening."

"Aha! You admit it. You're after my recipe."

He closed the distance between them, backing her into a corner between the sink and refrigerator. A hand on either side boxed her in. "Really?"

She pressed both palms against his chest, felt the leap of his pulse and experienced a ripple of excitement as she gazed into smoldering, dark eyes.

"If you think all I want from you is a recipe, lady, you're way off base." He trailed a row of kisses from her chin to her ear. Then as her head dipped to one side, he followed the long cord that throbbed furiously along her neck.

Something like lightning slashed through Hallie's stomach. Her knees buckled, and the edge of the counter creased her back as he pressed against the length of her. Feverishly she dug her fingers into the fabric of his shirt. It was a feeble effort at best. Soon she was beyond any defense, caught up as she was in last night's fantasy. She returned his kisses until the room slid from focus and bells pealed in her ears.

Chino eased back, his breathing ragged. For a moment, he rested his forehead against hers. Proving a point was one thing; this was something else. "Shouldn't you answer your telephone?" His smile was lopsided.

Hallie flexed her fingers in his shirtfront, her face blank.

He raised her chin with one finger, kissed her again and murmured, "What is that chili ingredient you guard so fiercely, hmm?"

The telephone stopped ringing and clicked to her answering machine. His words, not the garbled mutter of the taped message, cut through Hallie's confusion. "I should have known." Releasing his shirt, she ducked beneath his arm. "You haven't changed one bit. You're still an arrogant jerk."

"Hey, it was a joke, okay?"

She crossed her arms and glared. Only a fool would believe that.

Chino shook his head. "Oh, brother. Someone else hasn't changed. You're still..." He was going to say naive, until he looked at her with her hair tumbled from his fingers, her lips dewy from his kisses and her eyes slightly unfocused. She looked more innocent than naive. And his old need to protect her hadn't diminished—no matter how badly he wanted her—and oh, how he wanted her. But he'd be damned if he'd fight with her. Not about the past and not about the present.

"Hell," he growled, "I'm leaving. When you want a civilized conversation about what to expect in Fort Worth, call me. Until then be advised—the old man cheats at chess."

Remorse hit Hallie the moment he'd gone. Why couldn't she keep her dealings with him impersonal? But she had only to look at his violets to find her answer. Chino Delgado triggered volcanoes of emotion within her. He always had. Very likely he always would. Yet they were as different as sulfur and sandpaper, and the sparks that resulted each time they came together had the same outcome as striking a match. Was any building, even one as historic as the Cellar, worth all this emotional upheaval?

The Cellar was still on her mind as she showered and dressed for her visit with Chino's father. Perhaps she should let Chino turn it into a glass-fronted chain restaurant like all the others. No, the Cellar *was* important. And the possibility that she might never see him again if she stepped aside seemed unbearable. All these years when she thought she'd put him out of her heart, he'd been there. Buried deep. Mired in rejection and sorrow, but there all the same.

Gram had always said the Lord worked in mysterious ways. Surely this qualified. If she didn't confront the past, overcome the profound rejection she'd felt when he'd left her in that loft, she might never enjoy a normal relationship. Hallie realized that when push came to shove, she was no different from Evie and Glynnis. She wanted marriage to go with her cottage and white picket fence, too.

On her way to see Ram, she mulled it all over and couldn't help a grin at her own expense. Leave it to her to do things backward! Marriage was supposed to spark the desire for a cottage and white picket fence, not the other way around.

Ram Delgado was in bed this time when Hallie walked into his room. She was instantly concerned about his gray pallor, not to mention the presence of a nurse, oxygen tanks and other medical paraphernalia ringing his bed. "Mr. Delgado," she said in a hushed voice, "what's wrong?"

A pretty dark-haired nurse answered, "He's had a setback. Didn't they tell you at the desk? Only family may visit."

Hallie shook her head. "I didn't stop there. We spoke earlier. I assumed I could come up, same as before."

"You can," he said briskly. "Medical folks get upset at the least little flutter of a man's ticker."

"Fibrillations and shortness of breath are not little things in a man who's had two previous angioplasties." The nurse was equally brisk.

Hallie saw his jaw lock in a stubborn set reminiscent of Chino's. "When did this happen?" she asked. "I don't think Chino knows. I'm sure he doesn't," she revised. "He only left my house a short time ago."

Just then the door flew open and two men rushed in. One, who seemed to be the younger, wore a three-piece suit, the other jeans and a sweat-stained work shirt. Both bore the unmistakable dark good looks of the Delgados. Hallie stepped aside to give them room, unsure which two they were.

"Dad?" The men spoke in unison before the one in the suit turned to the nurse applying electrodes to Ram's bare chest. "Dr. Coulter called Babs. Why haven't you moved him into intensive care, Martha, if they've scheduled a bypass?"

"Cody," the older of the men said, "save the grilling tactics for the courtroom. Martha knows what she's doing."

The younger man didn't look convinced. He wheeled, hands bracketing his slim waist, and spied Hallie lurking in the shadows. "Who are you?"

"Leave her be," the man on the bed said weakly. "She's a friend."

"Since when?" scoffed Cody. He exchanged dark glares with his father.

Hallie felt heat skim her cheeks. Did all the Delgados jump to conclusions? "I'm Hallie Bergstrom," she said evenly. "I came to play chess." She stepped between the newcomers and patted Ram's hand. "Chino said you cheat. I expect to find out for myself. You wouldn't stand a girl up, would you?"

He flashed her a semblance of the cocky Delgado grin. "Never have and don't intend to start now. Give me a week, darlin'."

"Okay." She squeezed his fingers and turned to leave.

The huskier and older of the two sons followed her to the door. "Under the circumstances, I think you'd better check with one of us before you visit."

She met his harsh gaze and saw something she didn't like. "What circumstances are those?"

"You challenge one Delgado, you challenge us all."

"Group chess? How innovative. I assume you make your own rules?"

He gripped her elbow and escorted her out. "Save the cute quips. None of us like the way you're messing up Chino's head. Nor do we appreciate your playing on Dad's sympathies because you remind him of our mother. He's an old man with a weak heart. Do I make myself clear?"

Hallie jerked her arm free. Lifting her chin and squaring her shoulders, she walked away. She wouldn't dignify his ludicrous accusations with an answer. But blast it, she was worried about Ram. And she wanted to feel free to call and find out how he was after surgery—which was why she wouldn't bicker with whichever son didn't have the courtesy to tell her his name before he lit into her. Although from his age, she guessed it must be Jesse. If so, he was the head of the family while Ram was in the hospital. Hallie knew what it was like dealing with a family crisis. Another reason for not getting embroiled in a confrontation.

Her head was down when she pushed through the heavy front door. She almost missed seeing Chino coming at a dead run up the steps—would have missed him had they not collided. "Oof." The small sound escaped, along with her breath.

"Hallie?" Chino stopped and gripped both her hands in his. "I just got home. Babs told me about Dad. Her call was the one we missed."

"Chino. I'm sorry. I didn't play any messages back before I came here. You know about his bypass, then?"

He nodded, and she felt the slight tremor that passed through his body. Stepping closer, she laid one palm against his cheek. "It'll be all right, Chino. He's tough."

"How touching," sneered a slender woman who stopped on the step below Chino. She flicked a small piece of lint from an immaculate navy suit.

Hallie backed away, but Chino didn't release her hands. "Hello, Serita. What are you doing here?"

"Babs sent me out to find you, Chino. And naturally I'm terribly concerned about my father-in-law."

"Former father-in-law," Chino said curtly. "Why the sudden interest?"

She joined him on the step and placed a hand on his arm. "Babs and I are best friends, Chino. You know that. Can't you let bygones be bygones?"

Hallie yanked away from his hold. Unlike Serita's perfect nails, hers were broken from scrubbing cast-iron chili pots and gardening; not even a stiff brush had cleaned all the dirt from beneath them. As well, Chino and Serita still made a striking couple. Ice seemed to form in her stomach. Muttering goodbye to Chino and something less distinct to Serita, Hallie took flight. She didn't heed his efforts to call her back.

Driving home, she couldn't help but speculate about the demise of his marriage. Serita sounded like a woman who wanted a second chance. With her and Penny Beth buzzing around like those honeybees Mama Claire had mentioned, it was a wonder Chino had strength enough left for kissing anyone else.

Hallie ran a finger over her lips in memory. Granted, she didn't know a whole lot about the quality of kisses, but in her opinion Chino hadn't held much back. She didn't, however, have any desire to be one of a bevy. Let Chino keep a whole hive if he wanted. She would call Ivy Delgado and keep tabs on Ram that way.

Which she did that very afternoon, and found he was scheduled for surgery in the morning. Ivy promised to call the moment he came out of recovery. She suggested Hallie wait with them at the hospital, but Hallie declined. Obviously Ivy didn't know how others in the family felt.

Glynnis dropped by for coffee the next morning. "I got a letter from Joe Bonner yesterday," she said, fidgeting with her cup. "Must be true what they say about absence making the heart grow fonder."

"A letter?" Hallie stopped, cup halfway to her mouth. "That's great. How's he doing? Nothing wrong with his mother, I hope."

Glynnis chuckled. "That's what I like about you, Hallie. I told Evie last night, and she all but has me buying a gown and picking out churches. His mom's fine. He's working a lot of hours, but I think he misses Cedarville. He sounds lonely."

"I'm sure. Dallas is fast-track living."

"Would you mind terribly if I took some time to visit him when we go to your cook-off in Fort Worth?"

"Not at all." Hallie missed the dreamy look in her friend's eyes. "You can use my truck. I'm getting Gram's tent-trailer spiffed up. I'll bring a good book with me. I'll tell Evie to bring one, too."

"Thanks, Hallie. You're a true pal. Well, I'd better finish this run before my muscles seize up. I've been lazy lately."

"I'll call you later in the week about the time. It'll be easier with the trailer."

"Have you heard from Chino since you beat him?"

Hallie waved a hand at the violets. "He brought those." Then she told Glynnis about his father. "So," Hallie finished, "I'm not sure he'll go to Fort Worth. I imagine it depends on how the surgery goes."

"That's gotta be rough. Keep me posted, will you?"

Hallie nodded.

No sooner had Glynnis gone than the telephone rang. Hallie stared at it for a moment and offered a quick prayer for Ram before she picked it up.

"Hallie?" Ivy Delgado sounded tired.

"Yes. How is he?"

"He's in recovery. Only one of us can see him, and then only for a few minutes. We elected Jesse. Dr. Coulter did a five bypass. The damage was more extensive than they expected. But Ram's solid as a rock and otherwise in good health. Doc paints a rosy picture. Guess we'll just wait and see."

"I doubt his doctor would be so encouraging if he had reservations, Ivy."

"You're right, Hallie. Cody says I'm the world's worst pessimist. Like if I saw a red glow on the horizon, instead of admiring a beautiful sunset I'd think our house was burning."

"Come on, I'm sure you aren't that bad. Can I do anything to help? I'm not much on punching cows, but I could feed stock or baby-sit for Babs. If Jesse would let me, that is," she added quickly.

"I heard about what he said, Hallie. Not to excuse him, but he is under a lot of stress."

"I realize that, which is why I didn't smack him." She laughed to show she was kidding. "Please remember, if there's anything I can do, call me."

"Invite Chino over for dinner tonight," Ivy said in a low voice. "I'll be more than happy to relay the invitation."

"Wouldn't it be better if I fixed something for everyone and brought it out to the ranch? I could do fried chicken, cold salads and brownies."

"That's not it," Ivy murmured. "Serita's becoming a nuisance. She just got Babs to invite her to dinner tonight. And I can tell Chino's desperate to get away."

Hallie gnawed at her lower lip. "Are you sure about this, Ivy?"

"Positive. What time should he be there?"

"Ah . . . seven, I guess."

"Good. He'll bring the wine."

Hallie stared at the receiver for several moments after Ivy hung up. This was not a bright thing she'd done. Not after the way they'd parted yesterday. She should call Ivy back and refuse. As she reached for the phone, it rang. Fearing something had happened to Ram, she grabbed it up. "Yes?"

"Just tell me this," Chino said. "Did Ivy twist your arm?"

Hallie didn't know quite what to say.

"That's what I figured," he retorted. "Forget it. You're off the hook."

"No, Chino, wait." Hallie found her voice. "I offered to bring food out to the ranch for everyone. She said you could use a break from the family. But if you'd rather not come..."

"I would. Very much," he said softly. "White or red wine?"

"White. Oh, and do you like chicken?"

"Not much I don't like. And I swear, Hallie, I won't mention chili."

"Fair enough. See you at seven." This time when she replaced the receiver, she was smiling.

Hallie planned a relaxed dinner. Not that she'd entertained many men before. But the fact was, she was a good cook, thanks to Gram. It was the conversation part that worried her. One might think an English teacher would have enough command of the language to converse with anyone. Not true, especially if one ruled out subjects they had in common—such as chili, the Cellar and high school. Before Hallie decided on a safe opening, it was five to seven and he was knocking on her back door.

"How's your father?" she asked, accepting the bottle of chilled wine.

Chino grinned. "Well enough to be giving orders and making demands. When I left he was going ten rounds with the nurse—Martha—over a bedpan. She's half his size, but there was no doubt in my mind who was going to win. Wow, something smells great. I didn't know I was so hungry."

"That's how I was when Gram was in the hospital the last time. It's nerves. If you open the wine, I'll dish up our food. I thought we'd eat on the screened porch. It's cooled by ceiling fans and is quite pleasant in the evenings."

"Anything suits me. I considered going to Bob's for a steak. Except a restaurant would have been harder to explain to the family. I hope you don't mind, Hallie, but I left your number with the hospital in case they need me."

"Of course I don't mind. Come on, let's eat." She led the way, carrying a full tray. When he tried to take it, saying it was too heavy for her, she refused.

After their plates were filled and Chino had given a short toast complimenting her on the great-looking dinner, he suddenly asked, "Did Ivy tell you Serita's been bird-dogging me all day?"

Hallie buttered a roll, not knowing if she should give Ivy away or not.

"I don't normally talk about the women I've been involved with, but I couldn't help thinking you left with the wrong impression yesterday."

Hallie's head came up. She burned him with her gaze. "I don't know what to believe. I remember all the lies you told your friends about me."

He tossed his napkin over his silverware and ran his fingers down his wineglass. "Look," he said, avoiding her eyes, "I didn't tell lies about scoring with you that night." He gave a small shrug. "I just didn't say anything. I'm not proud of it, but I can't change things." Nor could he bring himself to admit she'd had him running scared that night.

"It hurt me a lot, Chino," she said simply, also fiddling with her wineglass. This time, she averted her gaze.

"Don't." He reached over and clasped her hand. "The last thing I ever wanted to do was hurt you. Why in God's name do you think I left?"

Hallie eased her hand away. "We'd better eat before it gets cold. I told myself all afternoon that there were three topics off limits. Chili, the Cellar and our past. You were about to tell me why I was mistaken about your relationship with Serita." She stabbed at her salad with her fork.

He cleared his throat. "There is no relationship. There never was. I'm not proud of that, either." Chino wasn't sure how much of the truth Hallie was ready to hear. He ate a piece of chicken and wondered what he should reveal. "I went to a graduation party after leaving you. Really tied one on. By morning, I had a wife. I don't remember it, but Serita had the paper. She wanted a rich rancher, and she was furious when I refused to join Dad and Jesse. I knew for a year she was running around on me. If she hadn't filed, I would have, after finals. Her second husband was rich, but smart. When he died suddenly, she discovered that a prenuptial agreement gave the ranch to his kids. She married number three before two's epitaph was even dry. Seems the bank owned his spread. I honestly don't know why she's back hitting on me. So there you have it in a capsule. I just want to stay out of her way."

Hallie cleared their dinner plates and brought coffee and brownies with ice cream. "Did you tell her how you feel, Chino?"

"More than once. But she and Babs go way back. My sister-in-law has a heart of gold and not a brain in her head. If Jesse didn't have so much on his shoulders at the ranch, I'd prevail on him to intervene. But with Dad and all—" His sentence was cut off by the telephone.

Hallie jumped to answer it, not liking the worry that flickered in Chino's eyes. She said hello several times before hanging up in frustration. "I know someone was there. Maybe you should call the hospital."

He did and found out Ram was stable. No one had called.

Hallie made light of the incident, and they retired to the living room with second cups of coffee.

"I'm stuffed." Chino rubbed his stomach and stretched. "Good dinner."

The telephone jangled again. She took it in the hall. Same story. The line was open but silent. Hallie saw no need to mention the frequency of the wrong numbers—or crank calls—to Chino. Instead, she asked about his historic old home in San Antonio. They went on to discuss the economy and the whereabouts of people they both knew. The phone shrilled a third time, and Hallie broke off in the middle of a sentence.

"Let me get it," Chino insisted. "If it's a crank caller, it won't hurt to let him think you have a man in the house."

She acquiesced. But the result was the same, and Chino questioned her.

"The crank calls started with Penny Beth's story," she admitted reluctantly. "I kind of figured it for your friends, Chino."

"It's harassment," he snapped. "No friend of mine would do such a thing. But I'll sure as hell ask around. Do they ever speak?"

"At first. Following the chili challenge. Not since Buzzard Flats, now that I think about it."

He looked thoughtful. "Maybe you should get an unlisted number."

"And knuckle under to some creep? No way." She avoided his steady gaze. "Maybe if they don't stop after Terlingua, I'll consider it, okay?"

"When are you leaving for Fort Worth?"

"I'm not sure. Are you going?"

"Depends on Dad. I'll go if he's out of danger." He caught her yawning. "Why didn't you tell me I was overstaying my welcome?"

"I didn't sleep well last night," she mumbled. Although she'd be darned if she'd tell him why.

"Let me help with the dishes, then I'll leave."

She laughed, a genuine laugh. "Funny, but I've never pictured you up to your elbows in dishwater. I don't have a dishwasher, you know."

"My first restaurant, I cooked, served and washed dishes. I'm a fair cook, too. Someday you'll have to come to San Antonio and I'll prove it."

"Someday I'd like to see your house. I have a weakness for old homes."

Chino looked at the sparkle in her eyes, and suddenly he had a weakness for *her*. He took a step toward her, but she retreated. "What?" he asked, rubbing a hand over the back of his neck. "No good-night kiss?"

"Don't spoil a nice evening, Chino. Every time you kiss me, we end up having a colossal argument."

"Sometime we'll have to analyze why. I'm going to begin again with you, lady. If we both get to Fort Worth, I'd like to show you around. Dallas has a chili museum I think you'd enjoy, and you haven't seen any of my restaurants."

"I don't know." Hallie worried her lip. "Should I trust you?"

His eyes darkened. "Why not?" He moved toward her again.

She walked to the door and opened it. "Because I don't think you're kidding about wanting to know what's in my chili. I think you're used to having things your own way. Women melt into little puddles at your feet, Chino, and I'm no exception. I'm serious about saving the Cellar, but to you everything's a game. We'll see how you feel when this chili thing is all over."

"That's crazy." He waved a hand in the air. "I don't give a damn what you put in your chili. I explained to you why I want to win. Chili's my livelihood, and it's part of the family history."

She smiled. "I rest my case, Chino. Good night. Tell Ram I'll visit after I win in Fort Worth." Gently, she shoved him out and closed the door.

He hammered a few times, then gave up.

The telephone rang as she heard the crunch of gravel beneath his boots. Hallie lifted the receiver, wishing she could get him back. But his truck lights already were bobbing down the lane. All at once she found the silence on the other end of the line unnerving. "Who is this?" she asked frantically. For a moment she heard breathing, then a click. Goose bumps rose on her arms.

Maybe these calls were connected with the chili cook-offs.

Hallie shivered. The question was—did Chino know more than he let on? Whether he did or not, she'd better keep her eyes open once she got to Fort Worth.

CHAPTER FIVE

THROUGHOUT THE WEEK, Hallie periodically checked with Ivy to see how Ram Delgado was progressing.

"It's amazing," Ivy said Thursday morning. "He's doing far better than anyone anticipated. You should be able to visit him by the time you get back from Fort Worth."

"How did you know I was going to Fort Worth?"

"Silly." Ivy laughed. "The men at our house have been talking chili seasonings and cooking strategy since you beat Chino in Buzzard Flats. I told you, it's a big deal to them. So big, Kirby's flying up there to offer Chino moral support. Beware, Hallie."

Hallie thought about the calls she'd been receiving at odd hours all week and shivered. "How wary should I be?" she asked. "Have you heard of things happening?"

"Things? Hallie, the tone of your voice gives me the shivers. I meant that tongue-in-cheek. Are we talking something specific?"

At the sharpness in Ivy's voice, Hallie backed off. "It was your warning. I was only playing along, Ivy. Remind me not to spar with an attorney again." Nice as Ivy was, Hallie decided, she was still a Delgado. When it came down to it, Hallie didn't know her well enough to trade confidences.

Ivy laughed again. "I hear that all the time from Babs and Louisa. They say I make a federal case out of the least little thing."

"Who's Louisa?" Hallie hadn't heard the name before.

"Kirby's fiancée. She's from Spain. Nice lady, but her English isn't up to my jokes. And Babs, bless her heart, just doesn't catch on."

"Ah, so Kirby's breaking tradition? No blonde for him."

"What makes you say that?" Ivy sounded amused. "Actually Louisa's strawberry blond. And all the women in her family are drop-dead gorgeous. You didn't see Kirby with a brunette, did you? Louisa has a temper to go with that Madrid-red hair."

"It's nothing really," Hallie murmured. "One of my friends commented once that women bleached their hair to fit the Delgado image. I don't know why I mentioned it. Chino fell out of step when he married Serita."

"Yes, but that didn't last," Ivy mused. "I hadn't thought about it in those terms before. But we're all very different. Come to think of it, their mother's hair was almost the exact shade of yours. Say, you'd fit right in!"

"Not me!" Hallie felt the heat rise in her cheeks. She coughed and cleared her throat. "It was just an observation, Ivy. Really, I've kept you too long. Tell Ram how pleased I am he's getting along so well. Let him know I'll call next week to see if he's up to a game of chess."

"I probably shouldn't tell you, Hallie, but I think he's practicing. He badgered Jesse for his old car set. One where the pieces are on pegs so he can't drop them off the bed. And don't you dare tell him I ratted."

Hallie smiled to herself. "I won't. I've noticed he does like winning. On the other hand, a lot can be said for the healing effect of determination."

"I hope you're right. Hey, I hear Cody stomping around trying to find something in the kitchen. I'd better go before he has everything out on the counters. Good luck in Fort Worth, Hallie. We'll talk later."

"Sure. And thanks." Hallie clicked off, but snatched the receiver up again and dialed Evie. She hadn't heard from her all week and wanted to tell her exactly when they'd leave in the morning. Evie's phone rang for a long time before someone picked it up and croaked a word that passed for hello.

"Evie, is that you?"

"I'b god a bad code," the hoarse voice replied, punctu-ating the announcement with a series of sneezes.

"Bad isn't the half of it. You sound terrible. No wonder you haven't called. I guess this means you won't be going tomorrow."

Evie said something froggy.

Hallie took it to mean no. "Are you taking medicine?"

Another croak, which Hallie translated as yes. "Do you need anything? Juice? Chicken soup? A good book?"

"I'b god enuff. Keeb away."

"Not on your life. I'm going to make you some of Gram's chicken soup. I'll set it by your door, ring the bell, then wait in my car until I see you pick it up. And that's final."

"You should be a mudder." With that statement, Evie signed off.

The moment Hallie had hung up, she called Glynnis. As soon as she answered, Hallie demanded to know if she was aware of Evie's condition.

"Hello to you, too," Glynnis chuckled. "Yes. I knew. She made me promise not to tell. You know Evie. Ms. Compulsive-Obsessive was afraid you'd cancel on her ac-count. I told her I'd skip visiting Joe."

"You most certainly will not baby-sit me and miss a date. Not everyone cooking chili has a cheering section. There were singles at the last one."

"How many had friends who got them into it, though?"

"Point taken," Hallie said dryly. "But never mind, I'll pick you up at eight. When we get there, you'll visit Joe as planned. I know you want to."

"If you really mean that, Hallie, we need to swing by the Cellar. Joe left a couple of personal boxes in the back room. I said we'd bring them."

"No problem. I've been wanting to see if Chino's keep-ing his word about leaving things at the Cellar the same. Do you think they still serve espresso? If so, I'll have a double mocha for breakfast."

"The place smells like chili. I met with the parents of my thespian group there the other night. I had a chili dog with my usual *latte*."

Hallie was glad Glynnis couldn't see the face she'd made. "Could you be a little more conventional at breakfast?"

Glynnis laughed. "Sure. I'll skip the *latte* and get a bowl of Hellfire and Damnation Chili for the road. See you at eight, Classy Lassie."

Hallie frowned as she headed for the kitchen to begin her chicken soup. Chino certainly hadn't wasted any time installing his chili pots. Just then, she remembered her secret ingredient. Last night she'd heard noises outside and had stored it in an old margarine tub in her freezer.

She was getting paranoid. Twice, she'd gotten up and flipped on all the lights. Quite frankly, she felt stupid, since nothing had seemed amiss. She couldn't *prove* the phone calls were connected to the cook-offs. It could be some nutcase who'd memorized her number.

Setting a pot of vegetables on to simmer, she swore that if it happened again after Fort Worth, she'd go down and talk with Cedarville's police chief.

FRIDAY WAS ALREADY hot and sultry by the time Hallie pulled up in front of Glynnis's condo. While waiting for her friend to take her cat next door, Hallie applied a coat of sunscreen to the arm she tended to hang out the driver's window.

"Whew, is it a scorcher!" Glynnis remarked, climbing into the cab. "Think I'll make that an ice coffee for breakfast."

"Good idea," Hallie agreed. "You didn't say how big Joe's boxes are. Will we be able to lift them?"

"If not, I'm sure there'll be some muscle man willing to help. Chino's breakfast clientele has picked up considerably."

"Oh?" Hallie paused as she capped the sunscreen.

"Yeah. We'll probably have to wade through cowboys."

"So Chino *is* making changes."

Glynnis hesitated. "A few. Did you think he'd let it stay in the red?"

"Well, no. But everything in Cedarville is already so...so Western."

Glynnis rolled her eyes. "This is the heart of cowboy country, Hallie." She broke off. They'd arrived outside the Cellar and it was evident from the lack of parking space that with whatever changes Chino had made, business was definitely improving.

"I think I'll pull up to the back door," Hallie said when they'd circled the block twice. "We won't be long and it'll be easier loading Joe's boxes." Before Glynnis had a chance to comment, Hallie whipped down the alley. "Oh, no!" She slammed on her brakes. Chino's motor home was parked adjacent to the building. "There's no room to turn around."

"Guess you'll have to back out," Glynnis said matter-of-factly.

"Not me." Hallie shook her head. "I can't back this stupid trailer."

"It's bitty. You can see clear over it. What's so hard?"

"Then you do it," Hallie said. "I tried backing out of my driveway this morning. It wobbles. Didn't you notice one of the corners is crunched? I hit that big oak tree."

"Hallie! How'd you finally manage?"

"I went all the way to the garden fence. Scraped it, making the turn."

As they talked, a heavyset man wearing an apron and a cook's hat stepped out on the back stoop and lit a cigarette. "Hey, you," he yelled. "You! Lady! You can't park there. We're expecting a delivery any minute."

Hallie turned off the engine and climbed out. "I'll only be a minute. We're picking up a couple of boxes that belong to Joe Bonner. And we'd like two ice coffees to go."

"I'm telling you, you can't park here. The beef truck backs in. He'll cream you when he makes that last bend. Now vamoose."

"What's the trouble, Randy?" Chino pushed the screen door open. Except for rolled shirtsleeves, he was dressed like his cook.

Hallie smothered a laugh. So Mister Cool hadn't been kidding about doing dishes. Maybe she *had* misjudged him.

"Hallie?" Chino stepped out on the porch. "And Glynnis? What are you two doing lurking in my freight alley?"

"Boxes for Joe," Glynnis explained, digging for her dark glasses.

"Oh. Well, let me load them and we'll get you out of here before our beef arrives."

Glynnis dropped the smoked lenses over her eyes and waited, a smile playing at the corners of her mouth.

Hallie looked chagrined. She might have admitted to Chino's cook that she couldn't back out of his alley, but telling Chino was a different matter.

Missing the undercurrent, Chino solicited Randy's help.

"Glynnis, what'll I do?" Hallie hissed. "I swear, I can't back up."

Glynnis rubbed the side of her nose. "Swallow your pride. Ask Chino to move the darned thing."

Hallie knew she should. She considered it until they came out, each shouldering a box—showing off their muscles. It was a straight alley. Maybe if she waited until they went inside... Randy went in right away. Not Chino. He stood there, arms crossed. Waiting.

"Don't let us keep you, Chino." Hallie wiggled her fingers at him. "I'll just back out and give your beef free rein. See you in Fort Worth."

He nodded, but didn't move. Glynnis choked back a laugh.

Hallie climbed into the cab and motioned Glynnis to do the same. Then she closed her eyes and started backing.

"Whoa. Hey, hold it. Dammit! Stop!"

Hallie stood on the brakes, peeped out of one eye and saw that the trailer had turned left for no reason at all. It wasn't two inches from Chino's expensive rig.

"Pull forward again," he instructed. "I'll go back and guide you. Those little squirt trailers are sometimes a bear to back." Hallie blinked. He hadn't called her a dumb woman driver. He'd direct her, he said. Of course. How simple.

But it wasn't. He made circular motions with his arms. Hallie watched in the rearview mirror. Three times she spun her wheels the wrong way. At last, he held a palm out flat. She bit her lip and watched him approach.

"What's the problem, Hallie?" he asked mildly.

She gripped the wheel with sweating palms. "I can't seem to make it go straight. Would you mind doing it?" The last was barely audible.

"She hasn't driven with a trailer before," Glynnis offered helpfully.

Oh, boy. Hallie expected some sort of pompous lecture now. Instead, Chino studied her with dark, thoughtful eyes.

"If you're gonna drive a trailer, you better know how to back it. Glynnis, why don't you hop out? I'll get in and talk her through."

It was so easy, the way he explained things. When Hallie reached the end of the alley and parked on the street, she felt a surge of pride. Impulsively she hugged him. "I did it! Thanks, Chino, I . . . I don't know what else to say."

"Say you'll wait until we unload that beef truck. If you haven't driven with this trailer in a while, it might be wise if I followed you to Fort Worth."

"I've never had it out. It was Gram's. Your plan sounds good to me. I'll get Glynnis and we'll go have coffee. I want to see the place, anyway."

"I've . . . made a few changes."

She looked nettled. "How many? You said you wouldn't."

"Just look at them before you yell. Okay?"

She did, but with reluctance. And to her surprise, everything he'd done was tasteful. Authentic. She told him so when he came to collect them. "I really like the chandeliers, Chino. They fit right in."

"Glad you approve. Joe's mother had a book with pictures of the original interior. A craftsman in San Antonio was able to duplicate them. In fact, I'll bring it, and you can take a look at it later. Are you ready?"

They were. The seven-hour trip to Fort Worth breezed by. It was comforting to Hallie to see Chino in her rearview mirror. After the way he'd handled her backing up, she didn't doubt that he could help her in any crisis.

Something else occurred to her as they followed the signs to the cook-off. Life was infinitely nicer when they weren't fighting.

The Fort Worth site turned out to be a beautiful park. A welcome change from Buzzard Flats. "This is more like it," Hallie murmured. "I think I'm going to enjoy the weekend. Too bad Evie's missing it."

"There's Joe," Glynnis said, blushing. "I forgot to tell you he was coming for me. I didn't realize he'd be this early. Can you manage without me? I *could* stay." She seemed nervous.

Hallie squeezed her friend's hand. "I'll be fine until you get back. What could possibly go wrong between now and then?"

Still Glynnis dallied. She made an issue of helping Hallie choose a spot beneath a large shade tree, near a manmade pond.

Shade wasn't a problem here, and Hallie was quick to point that out.

Chino needed hookups that Hallie's small trailer didn't. He parked just across the clearing, then joined them, suggesting he and Joe help pop Hallie's tent out. Never having done it before, she didn't argue. As it was, the men had to read the directions three times to figure out how the awning worked, and by the time they finished it was nearly dusk.

"You two staying for the dance?" Chino asked Joe. In the distance, a lively Western band was tuning up.

Glynnis busied herself arranging Hallie's stove and her pots and pans on a folding metal table Chino had set up beneath the awning.

Hallie noticed Joe staring at the slender woman as if waiting for her to answer. "Just leave that, Glynnis," she said. "I think Joe must be hungry."

Chino's glance darted between the two. Both turned red. He slapped Joe on the back. "Hey, it's just a dance. No big deal." Turning to Hallie, he said, "We'd have to use your truck, but we could catch a bite in Dallas and then take in that chili museum I mentioned."

Hallie ran an eye over the campsites that were rapidly filling up. She wasn't sure about leaving her trailer unattended.

Evidently Chino sensed that. "Chili-heads can get a little rowdy at times. But basically they're honest."

It was his open smile that decided her. "Sure, why not? I haven't been to Dallas for ages, and I'd like to look over Fort Worth, too. Glynnis, if you two don't already have set dinner plans, why don't you join us?"

Joe slipped an arm around Glynnis's waist. "I'm cooking tonight." He smiled down into her eyes. "Grab your overnight case and we'll take off."

Glynnis flushed and hurried to Hallie's pickup. Joe said goodbye for both of them, caught up to Glynnis and hugged her as they walked to his car.

Shocked, Hallie gaped after them. She felt foolish with all her talk about being fine until Glynnis got back. Her friend wouldn't *be* back tonight. She'd obviously come prepared to spend the night with Joe. Hallie hoped Glynnis knew what she was doing. She'd hate to see her get hurt.

Chino noticed her concern and mistook it for disapproval. "What? Are you so antimen that you begrudge her having a relationship?"

"I'm not antimen," Hallie refuted. "Who told you that?"

He lifted her trailer from the pickup and tightened the ball back on the hitch before he answered. "You don't date any locals. Word around Cedarville's singles circuit is that you don't like men, period."

"That's not true." She crossed her arms defensively. "I'm just selective. And I'm not going to dinner with you if we're spending another evening assassinating my character."

He held up both hands. "No, ma'am. Nary a potshot." He hustled her into the passenger seat, helped himself to her keys, and began talking about other things. Along the way, he pointed out several of his Chili Houses and related some amusing stories about getting the chain started. "Things are going pretty well now," he admitted with a casual shrug.

"They look plenty busy," she observed. "You know, Chino, I don't have any objection to your expanding in Cedarville. But it's not the right image for the Cellar."

He removed a hand from the wheel and linked their fingers. "Remind me to show you that book when we get back to the park. What would you think if I restored the whole building as closely as possible to the original interior?"

Her heart did a funny flip. "And do what with it?"

"A Chili House. What else? It's my business, Hallie."

"And what about your word being your bond? Or is that only true if you win and get what *you* want?"

He shot her a glance. "I see." His tone was clipped. "I thought you'd be pleased. However, I can see you don't want me owning the Cellar at all."

Tension inside the truck thickened. "Now you're putting words in my mouth. I just don't like being manipulated. It makes me wonder how far you'll go to win," she said unhappily.

Chino thought she was blowing his remarks all out of proportion and told her so. "Under the circumstances, let's eat at a steak house, shall we? Lord knows I wouldn't want to have you misconstrue my taking you to one of my restaurants tonight." Talk after that was stilted, even though during dinner he kept to safe subjects like football.

On leaving the steak house, Hallie remarked offhandedly that it was a beautiful moonlit night.

"A perfect night for lovers," Chino muttered. "Not much for us to discuss there."

Hallie clammed up at once. They entered the chili museum in complete silence and she wondered why they'd come. He stalked ahead and she hung back, reading placards about all the big cook-off winners—which included his father and brothers, of course. The absence of Chino's name suddenly seemed terribly significant to Hallie. Why else, in his present mood, would he bring her here?

When she asked him, Chino ignored the question. "I'm ready to leave. What did you want to see in Fort Worth?" he snapped as they hit the interstate.

She blinked back angry tears. "Nothing. We can go back to the park if you'd like."

"It's your call."

She faced front, fingers laced in her lap. "Maybe we should bottle this spontaneous combustion for the cook-off." Her attempt at humor failed.

"By all means, since that seems to be the most important thing to you."

"I didn't dream up this contest, Chino."

"Nor did I. You think I like the ribbing I get at work? It was bad enough when it was just my family."

"Speaking of family," she said, "I forgot to ask about Ram. How is he?"

"And that's another thing—you and Dad! Don't be too quick to think you've found a rich old man with one foot in the grave and the other on a banana peel. The doc says he may outlive us all."

"Stop it, Chino. That's hateful. If I had a father, which I don't, I'd want him to be like yours. He's got a great sense of humor. He's proud to pieces of his family, in spite of his bluster. I know how worried you are..." She was relieved to see the park. "Ah, here we are. Let's call it a night before we say things we'll both regret later."

"Good idea." Chino pulled her truck into the space between their two campsites, yanked out the keys and deposited them in her lap.

Before Hallie could thank him for dinner, he got out and slammed the door. She might have tried one last time to mend the rift had the door to his motor home not opened and a younger, stockier version of him stepped out. Kirby Delgado, she guessed. Beyond him, a willowy redhead—and Penny Beth Frazier. Ivy hadn't said Penny Beth was included.

Hallie felt a swift stab of jealousy. She averted her gaze as she went through the motions of locking her truck. Then she stumbled through the dark to her tent-trailer.

In the next site a campfire burned brightly. Hallie felt better until the three men seated there, drinking beer, broke off talking and eyed her progress. Something about them, their scruffy beards maybe, raised the hair on the back of her neck. Her uneasiness remained even after she'd lit a butane lantern and got out her book. Talk and laughter drifted through her screened windows, underlining her loneliness. She took off her boots and curled up on the bunk. Soon her eyelids felt heavy; she reached over to turn off the light. Campfires were burning low and conversations winding down when Hallie remembered that she'd left her secret ingredient in her truck. She was about to pull on her boots and go out to get it just as she overheard one of the men next door mention Chili Man.

Hallie strained to hear. *Not nice,* she chided herself. Then, as Gram used to say of all eavesdroppers, Hallie truly got an earful.

"So Chili Man wants the chick outa commission?" someone with a rough, deep voice growled.

"Shh," warned another. "You know he needs this win bad. Cook-offs ain't no place for women, anyway."

"Yeah," the other two chimed in, then all three laughed.

Hallie's blood chilled. What did it mean? Were they discussing *her?* Of course they were. She lay staring blindly at the corrugated metal roof. It was as if they wanted her to hear—to scare her. She took a deep breath. They couldn't possibly know her secret ingredient was in the truck. And there were people all around. She pulled the sleeping bag up over her ears to block out their voices and made herself think about the patience Chino had exhibited in teaching her to back the trailer. No. She didn't really believe Chino would wish her harm. It was just talk.

Next morning, in the clear light of day, Hallie was forced to revise her thinking. Up at five-thirty to slow-cook her chili, Hallie went to light her stove and discovered the white gas had been drained onto the ground.

She shot a menacing glance toward Chino's still-dark motor home. That was a mean thing to do. Good thing she had a spare canister. Two, in fact.

Except that when she went to get them they weren't where she'd packed them. Then she remembered Glynnis's saying they should be in an outside compartment for safety. Relief washed over her as she opened the niche and saw both red canisters still there.

The first one felt terribly light. Hallie turned it over and saw the spout was open. Snatching up the second tube, she wasn't surprised to find it in the same condition. It was then she noticed a dark mound at her feet and realized the air reeked of chili spice. How had she missed seeing the torn bags of her condiments all lying in a heap?

Anger exploded. Sleep like a baby, would he? She grabbed a small cast-iron skillet, rolled up her sleeves and marched across the clearing. Without regard for the hour she whammed on Chino's door. The state she was in, she didn't concern herself overly much with the dimpled marks it left. She'd dimple-mark his head if he wasn't too cowardly to show his face.

A sleepy-eyed woman opened the door a crack and loosed a string of fluid Spanish.

Hallie knew enough of the language to get the drift. Kirby's fiancée was not happy about being awakened at such an unholy hour. Tough. "You can tell that no-good, sneaking varmint to show himself." Hallie realized she was shouting when lights popped on and doors flew open all around.

Seeming thoroughly bewildered, the woman cracked the door wider. "Who, no-good varmint?" she asked.

"What is it, Louisa?" A tousled Chino set his sister-in-law aside, suddenly filling the doorway with his broad, bare shoulders.

If Hallie hadn't been so furious, she might have hyperventilated. His hair was mussed, matching a thatch of black curls on his chest arrowing straight down to blue jeans hastily donned and carelessly left partially open. She forced her gaze to his feet, which were also bare.

"Hallie?" Chino uttered her name around a muffled yawn. "What time is it? Did I oversleep?"

"Showdown time, you sneak," she shouted, not caring who heard. In the heat of emotion she swung her pan again. It glanced off the floor and accidentally smacked Chino's big toe.

He yelped and hopped around on one foot. "What in hell?" he growled. "Woman, are you demented?"

"Don't act innocent, you...you aardvark. Did you think I was so stupid I wouldn't know *you* had those guys drain my fuel?" She swung the skillet again, but this time he cleared the steps and grasped her arm.

By now they had an audience. One that appeared to be enjoying the show immensely.

Kirby replaced Chino in the doorway. In a mild tone, he suggested the principal parties step inside and be reasonable.

"Reasonable? *Reasonable?*" Hallie sputtered, heat flooding her cheeks. "Was it reasonable for him to let his goons dump all my spices into a molehill?" She wrenched away, leaving Chino holding the skillet.

"Hallie, I don't have the vaguest idea what you're talking about. If someone messed with your stuff, I swear I know nothing about it."

"Weasel. I heard them talking last night. I just didn't know what it meant—then."

"Them who?" He sounded distressed. "Know what *what* meant?"

Hallie turned and pointed, only to discover the space next to her trailer was vacant. "They're gone." She was puzzled. Then all at once she whipped around and glared at Chino. "Three men were in that space last night plotting about putting some chick out of commission—for you. This morning my fuel tanks are empty and my spices dumped. Now why would I assume they meant you? And me?"

She pulled her skillet from his lax fingers and lunged at him again. As he leapt aside, she hissed, "Hear this! I'm going to town for more spices. If anything—anything at all—is touched while I'm gone, you louse, I'll break both your kneecaps." She marched off toward her truck.

"Hallie, wait," Chino called. "I'll lend you spices. And gas."

The onlookers parted silently to let her through. As Chino followed, they gave teasing catcalls and poked fun.

By this time, Hallie was too furious to recognize that she'd been accepted into their ranks.

And Chino was too baffled by Hallie's accusations to give a damn about the crowd. Intent on making her listen, he forced his way through those assembled and landed hard on a sharp rock with a bare foot. By the time he recovered from the pain, her truck was out of sight. "Damn it all to hell!" Limping back to his rig, he closed his ears to the gibes made at his expense. As he reached his motor home, he said something succinct to Kirby, then both men disappeared inside.

When Hallie returned he was fully dressed and waiting impatiently by her table. His mood was black and dangerous.

She had her supplies—but her fury was unabated. Perhaps because she'd had to go to three different stores to find everything, and by the time she got back it was past the hour her chili should've been started. Chino's chili, meanwhile, was simmering away, lovingly tended by Penny Beth Frazier.

To Hallie that was the final insult. "Get out of my space," she ordered him.

No amount of arguing fazed her. She assembled her chili methodically, tuning Chino out as if he didn't exist.

Eventually he gave up and returned to his own area. Grim-faced, he asked Kirby if he'd seen anyone camped next to Hallie the night before. When his brother drew a blank, Chino took it upon himself to go from space to space asking the same thing. No one remembered, but Chino knew someone—or several someones—had been there because the coals were still warm.

As the afternoon waned, Hallie knew her chili wasn't ready to be judged. Refusing to withdraw, she filled a cup at the appropriate time and carried it up herself. It was no surprise to learn she didn't even place in the first of the two rounds.

What seemed horribly unfair was that in the final judging Chino took first place. Second went to a lady from Oklahoma, with white hair and a nice smile. Chino's arch rival, Habanero Hank, was less than thrilled with third. Having toughed it out to the end, Hallie turned away amid murmurs of sympathy. If it was vengeance she wanted, she got it—only a smattering of old-timers clapped when Chino's ribbon was awarded.

But Hallie didn't think that was fair, either. His chili was no less a winner because of her misfortune. After all, he might have won, anyway. She really didn't like hearing Hank leading the jeers. She'd never been a poor sport and she didn't intend to start now. A smile pasted on her lips, she congratulated Chino in a voice that carried.

"Hallie...I'm sorry," Chino said, catching her arm when she would have brushed past. "I'd give you my points if I could."

Dislodging his hand, she walked swiftly back to her unit and began stowing her gear. Almost everything was packed by the time Glynnis and Joe showed up. Fully prepared to pour heart and soul out to her friend, Hallie was stopped cold by their shocking news.

"We're getting married," Glynnis announced without prelude. "Look, Joe gave me his grandmother's engagement ring. Isn't it the most beautiful setting you've ever seen?" She smiled at Hallie. "Joe wants the ceremony to be in Dallas a month from today. Will you skip a cook-off to stand up with me, Hallie?''

Tears sprang to Hallie's eyes. She wasn't sure if they were tears of happiness for her friends or tears of frustration and pity for herself. All day she'd been on the verge of crying. Whichever, tears seemed the perfect close to a perfectly abominable weekend.

CHAPTER SIX

ON THE LONG DRIVE HOME from Fort Worth, Glynnis talked of nothing but wedding plans and Joe. At first Hallie didn't join in the conversation; her faith in men—one man in particular—had been shattered again. But she couldn't stay dispirited. Not when Glynnis bubbled over with such excitement.

"I know it seems like a sudden decision, Hallie, but I've wanted this for ages," Glynnis said for about the twentieth time that afternoon. "Do you think I'm making a mistake? You aren't saying much."

Hallie flashed her a genuine smile. "Who could get a word in edgewise?"

Glynnis stopped examining the lacy gold mounting of her ring and flushed. "I have been rambling, haven't I?"

"You're allowed."

The younger woman twisted the sparkling stone around on her finger. "Somehow, I always thought Evie would be the first of the three of us to marry. She's all talk, though. Not as experienced with men as she claims."

"Oh?" Hallie took her eyes from the road. "What gives you that idea?"

"Something she let slip when her guard was down. Four of her sisters are already married, and her family's pushing her. Evie brags a lot for their benefit. She hates holidays at home because they grill her constantly."

"I didn't know that. I've always thought she could pick and choose when it came to men. It makes me feel terrible, Glynnis. How can you be good friends with a person and not know these things?"

"Maybe for the same reason she didn't know you hadn't...well...and I have a theory about that. I think people hide the things that bother them most."

"Quite the psychologist, you with your degrees in art and drama," Hallie said, laughing. "I assure you, my lack of experience does *not* bother me."

Glynnis smiled sympathetically. "I'll bet on some level it does. Hey, we're at my place already. Oh, and it won't be home for long. Goodness, I haven't even told my family. Or Evie." Suddenly she seemed panicky.

Hallie set the emergency brake and gave her friend an impulsive hug. "It'll be fine, Glynnis. Everyone will be thrilled. Go in there and spread the joyous news. When Evie gets over her cold, the three of us will go shopping for your dress in San Antonio. I can practically see it. Satin and seed pearls."

Glynnis returned the hug. "*White* satin," she murmured, pulling away. She grasped Hallie's hand and said, "Joe and I didn't...well, what I mean is, it seems he's more traditional than I am. I was so nervous, but he was sweet. You and I are a lot alike in that respect, Hallie. I know you'll find a special man someday." She hugged Hallie again, then slipped out the door. Halfway to her apartment she turned and waved, her smile like a ray of sunshine.

All the way to her own house, Hallie mulled over what Glynnis had said. Those comments hit awfully close to home. Truth was, for years she'd dreamed of Chino Delgado riding in on a white charger and stopping outside her door just long enough to declare his undying love. How many times had she secretly planned her own wedding—always with Chino waiting at the altar? No matter how often or to whom she denied having feelings for him, Chino haunted her dreams.

Bumping to the end of her long driveway, she sat for a moment and stared at the well-tended garden made rosy in the setting sun. Gram had known. Or she'd guessed. Broken hearts weren't easy to hide. Funny, but Hallie felt like that again now—like she was wearing a fractured heart on her sleeve. Only this time Gram wasn't waiting inside with fresh berry pie and encouraging words. This time, Hallie Marie Bergstrom would have to heal herself.

Later, as she set about cleaning her chili pots under the outside faucet, she thought about something Gram had often reminded her of—that she came from tough Scandinavian stock. That her great-grandparents were immigrants who'd arrived with next to nothing and carved out lives in a harsh land. Gram had possessed that kind of strength. She'd left family and friends in Minnesota, trekking to faroff Texas because the man she loved had dreamed of striking oil. Hallie had asked once why she'd stayed in Texas after Grandpa Ola died, and Gram declared that all the Erickson women were like that. They loved once and forever.

Hallie carried her overnight bag in from the car. Did that still hold true, she wondered, if the last woman in the Erickson line loved a scoundrel? A sweet-talking scoundrel who put winning a chili cook-off above ethics.

Her telephone was ringing as she walked inside, and Hallie's stomach knotted. She didn't want to pick it up in case it was the *caller*. Just this moment her nerves were too raw. Deciding not to answer, she flipped the machine on to "listen" in time to catch the end of Ram Delgado's message.

"What in hell happened to you up there in the big city, darlin'?" he growled. "My sources were pretty sketchy. We need to talk."

Hallie doubted that. She didn't know who his "sources" were, but with two sons in the thick of it she figured he'd had a thorough accounting. Thorough and one-sided. At any rate, she wasn't up to rehashing it tonight. Tomorrow, if he was well enough, she'd visit him and recount her version. Face-to-face, she could gauge his reaction. Right now the only thing she was up to facing was bed, and if there was any justice in this old world she'd sleep till morning without dreaming of Chino.

Justice *did* exist. Hallie awakened to sunlight streaming through her white eyelet curtains. She lay there a moment, watching the sparkling dots dance across her floor as a morning breeze ruffled the fabric. Gram had once called the flickers of sunlight diamond rain. Wrapping her arms around her pillow, Hallie decided that any day beginning with diamond rain had to be good.

She hopped out of bed feeling more rested than she had in weeks, her spirits improved enough for her to sing in the shower as she washed her hair.

Right after that, Hallie was drying her hair in the morning sun out on the back porch when Chino drove in. Suddenly her brush stilled and she lost count of her strokes.

He climbed down from the cab, briefly met her gaze, then turned back and pulled out a giant stuffed panda. It filled his arms and hid his face.

Hallie straightened. Once again her heart forgot to listen to good sense and stepped up its pace. The stuffed toy reminded her how, in a weak moment near the end of the first year they'd met, she'd casually mentioned that as a child she'd longed for a panda bear. Next day a small one had mysteriously appeared in her locker. Of course Chino had denied any knowledge, but she'd known better. It still occupied a special place on her dresser.

He strode to within a foot of her toes and stopped, eyes suddenly clouded by emotion. He swallowed, glancing away toward the garden. He didn't speak.

Hallie rifled a nervous hand through her still-damp hair. Did he know how boyishly appealing he looked holding that potbellied bear with the big hind feet? Its bright red bow was a splash of color across a decidedly manly hand. But knowing the unscrupulous capability of that very same hand, she hardened herself against his appeal. Before she could collect her thoughts and suggest he leave, he threw her completely off balance.

"My mother used to sit on the porch and dry her hair in the summer, too. In winter she'd go inside by the fireplace. My brothers and I took turns brushing it while she read us stories. Summertime we were off riding horses or climbing trees, and she'd have to unsnarl it herself. She'd grumble about being abandoned, call us scalawags and say the Lord should have given her at least one girl. She never lived to meet any of her daughters-in-law.''

Something in his voice utterly destroyed the steel with which Hallie had meticulously girded her heart. ''How old were you when you lost her, Chino? I don't believe you've ever said.''

''I was twelve. Jesse was fourteen, Cody ten and Kirby almost nine.''

Hallie fiddled with her brush. They'd been so young. Younger even than she'd been when she'd lost her parents. Except they, at least, had Ram, and they hadn't lost home and friends in the process. ''Did your father hire a house-keeper?'' she asked, thinking it might have been harder on them to have a stranger in a home filled with such warm memories than for her to move in with Gram.

Chino propped a booted foot on the step below her and gave a shrug. ''A series.'' He smiled sheepishly. ''Jesse and I dreamed up all manner of ways to drive them off.''

''Why doesn't that surprise me?'' She sobered, leaning away from him.

''Look, Hallie.'' He held out a hand. ''We were just kids. It was our first experience with death, and we didn't under-stand it. I'm not a kid now. I didn't do any of those things that happened to you at the cook-off. I wouldn't. Damn it all, I lo—''

He broke off abruptly. Had he really almost said he loved her? Was it because of the talk about his mother? He shifted uncomfortably, accepting that it was true—love lying dor-mant for a long time had surfaced when he wasn't prepared for it. And judging by the stubborn set of Hallie's jaw, it was at a time when she wouldn't listen. Chino clamped down on his feelings.

''You what?'' she demanded.

''Never mind,'' he muttered. ''Just forget it. Frame of mind you're in, you wouldn't know the truth if it bit you.'' He pushed the bear at her, spun on his heel and stalked off.

"What's this for?" she yelled after him. "Should I check to see if he's ticking?"

He threw his reply back over one shoulder. "I had the crazy notion that you might look at him and believe any man who could cart a gift like that all the way through a Dallas mall deserved hearing out. I was wrong. Sleep with him, Hallie. Maybe he'll keep you warm nights. You sure won't let a man get that close."

"Not one as untrustworthy as you," she called. "Next cook-off, don't you dare come near my campsite. Do you hear me?"

"The next cook-off is the Chilympiad. I'm happy to say it's men only. If I win, I'll have all the points I need, and I won't have to cook again until the final." He swept off his Stetson and bowed. "So, Viva Terlingua, Hallie." In a flash he leapt into his truck and shot down her driveway.

"Showoff," Hallie muttered into the bear's furry head. A cold knot was building in the pit of her stomach. Somehow she hadn't thought about finishing the cook-off circuit without Chino.

She locked her arms around the big bear and rested her chin on the soft fur between his ears. Her drying hair fell in a curtain. First Glynnis's defection, now this. If Gram hadn't instilled in her the belief that a Bergstrom never gave up, she'd call it quits here and now.

Sighing, Hallie gathered up the panda and got to her feet. At least Evie was still in her corner. And the women's event in Luckenbach was coming up soon. If she could win that and place in one other event, she'd be much closer to saving the Cellar. Excluding the weekend of Glynnis and Joe's wedding, it was still possible to qualify for Terlingua before school started. Then maybe she could forget Chino Delgado and get on with her life.

Entering the house, Hallie carefully placed the panda in the center of her bed. Remembering Chino's prophecy, she threw herself on the bed and cradled the bear in her arms, proceeding to drench his fur with tears. As usual Chino was right. The bear was comforting. He was soft and filled her empty arms. Besides, he smelled faintly of Chino's after-shave. *Boy, she had it bad, sniffing a dumb bear.* Hallie un-wound her arms, stood and placed the stuffed toy in her grandmother's old rocker, where he looked as if he be-longed. All at once, she felt petty for not having thanked Chino. There was no excuse for bad manners.

Odd, but the crying left her filled with restless energy. Taking another page from Gram's book, Hallie directed the windfall toward a thorough housecleaning. Before lunch she waxed cabinets, cleaned tile with a brush, vacuumed cor-ners and washed windows. Afterward, she started on the outside, scraping the wooden trim and repainting it.

By nightfall her tiny home blossomed like new. Except that, by then, it hurt her to move. Nor had the work turned out to be the release she needed. Too many of her thoughts still centered on Chino Delgado—on his two sides she couldn't quite fuse into one man.

Too exhausted even to fix an evening meal, Hallie sat down to play the messages on her answering machine. Both Evie and Glynnis had called. And Ram Delgado—more than once. The last time he sounded upset that she hadn't returned his call. Hallie glanced at the clock. It was defi-nitely too late now. Tomorrow she'd run over to the hospi-tal, provided she could get out of bed, she thought ruefully as her telephone shrilled. She picked it up and promptly dropped it. Muscles that had wielded a paintbrush so long refused to function.

"Sorry," she said, scooping the phone up with her left hand. "I painted all day and my fingers don't want to work right."

Her explanation was met with silence. "Hello," she said, fighting a moment's panic. The breathing wasn't heavy, but it was there all the same. Hallie slammed the receiver down and started to unplug the phone. Reconsidering, she left it. In addition, she flipped on both front and back flood-lights. Uneasy, she rubbed a chill from her arms. Chino de-nied having any part in these so-called crank calls. She desperately wanted to believe him. But if not Chino, then who? And why?

Perhaps it wouldn't hurt to swing by the Cedarville police department on her way to visit Ram.

Twice in the dead of night Hallie's phone rang. Both times she bolted upright, her heart racing. Although willing to admit the calls were beginning to frighten her, she still refrained from bringing Chino's bear to bed.

But she slept until eight, and by then was almost too stiff to climb out of bed. The antics she went through to do simple things like button her blouse would have been laughable if they didn't hurt so much. Hallie cursed the cleaning frenzy—and the person ultimately responsible. Chino.

Since it didn't appear she'd be able to do much work, given the shape she was in, Hallie elected to go to town early. From the moment she set foot on her back porch, fury blinded her to residual pain. Fat red chili-pepper stickers completely covered her tent-trailer. It stood crimson in the morning sun, a veritable blanket of red broken only by bold, black pennants that read VIVA TERLINGUA.

"Oh, sure," she spat, "he's really outgrown childish pranks. Well, maybe he and Jesse got rid of housekeepers with stunts like this, but they don't scare me."

He'd made one glaring mistake yesterday—spouting "Viva Terlingua" as he left. He *must* have been responsible for this mischief. The proof was in the pudding—or in the peppers, one might say. Let the police handle him. Hallie didn't know much about law, but surely this came under the heading of malicious mischief.

That might well have been true anywhere but Cedarville. Half an hour later, she left the station fuming. Chief Potts and his deputy, as it turned out, were chili aficionados. The chief had even won the big one some years before. They couldn't have been more biased in favor of Chino if they'd come right out and said so. What they did say was that stickers were harmless—easily removed with a little elbow grease. The dolts were quite amused by her tales.

"Ooh, they make me furious!" Hallie bristled all the way to her truck. And if that experience wasn't humiliating enough, she was in such a hurry to leave she managed to get stopped for speeding right in front of the feed store, where Jesse Delgado was loading supplies on his flatbed truck.

Seething, Hallie drove off with greater care. She could well imagine being the topic of conversation at the Delgado dinner table tonight. A second speeding ticket would give them twice as much to laugh about.

And it wouldn't do to visit Ram until she cooled off. Instead, she headed for town to pick up a gift she'd ordered for him. With everything else it had slipped her mind that the department store had left a message on her machine saying the gift was in.

It was one in the afternoon before Hallie felt able to keep Chino's monkeyshines in perspective and not involve his father. Heeding Jesse's warning of two weeks ago, she stopped at the first-floor desk and gave her name. Surprisingly enough, she'd been cleared to visit.

Better yet, Ram was alone.

Hallie slipped into his room without knocking. "Hi," she said, happy to see him sitting up, looking well.

"So," the elder Delgado accused the moment he spied her, "you finally have a minute to visit a sick old man. Maybe *I* don't feel like company now."

"Is that so?" Hallie tossed back. "Then I guess you don't feel like checking out the gift I brought, either." She flashed the gaily wrapped package, then turned and reached for the doorknob.

"A present? What'd you get me? Shouldn't waste your money on an old geezer who's gonna kick the bucket any day. The kids'll just fight over it."

"Tsk, tsk. Don't we feel sorry for ourselves today? I suppose you badgered all your nurses until none of them will visit."

"Bah! What do you know? Smart-mouthed kid. Not even dry behind the ears. Wait till you get old and your offspring all desert you. Give me the present. May as well see what you spent your money on. Should've bought yourself a chili cookbook, instead. Why'd you screw up in Fort Worth?''

Hallie tipped her head to one side. "You're the one with all the spies. What did they tell you?" She placed the present on the narrow table used to serve meals and rolled it across his bed.

"Hmmph. Ivy's the only one who stops by regular. Have to pry everything out of her. All she said was Chino took first and you didn't place. Why don't you tell me what she left out?" He picked up the package and shook it all directions. When it didn't rattle, he shook harder.

"Ivy told it right. Chino took first and I didn't place. Are you going to open that thing, or are you going to shake it to pieces?"

He snapped the ribbon and ripped off the paper just like a kid.

Hallie hid a smile.

"Oh...lordy," he said, giving a little whistle as he lifted the lid on a walnut box. Gnarled, blunt-tipped fingers removed the folded board and lovingly caressed the intricately carved chess pieces nestled in blue velvet.

"They're magnetic," she was quick to point out. "My dad had a similar set that we used on vacations."

"Jesse brought me his old travel set. It has pegs on the pieces to poke in little holes. These old fingers are too clumsy to hit the damned things. Don't tell him, but the nurse got tired of picking 'em up. Battle-ax threw 'em in the trash."

"Watch who you're calling a battle-ax."

Hallie turned in time to see a vision in white stop beside the door. It was the nurse, the one Cody had called Martha. And if this woman weighed a hundred pounds, Hallie'd be surprised. She was somewhere between forty and fifty and very attractive. Surely not like anyone's image of a battle-ax!

Ram quickly closed the lid over his new chess set. It amused Hallie to catch him blushing like a teenager.

"Now, Martha," he mumbled, "just an old man's figure of speech. I didn't mean a thing by it. Honest, darlin'."

"Well," the woman said calmly, lifting his wrist to check his pulse, "see that you don't, you old reprobate, or I'll find the dullest needle in the packet to deliver your next shot. And tell your friend the truth. I threw them away because of your childish tantrums."

Hallie didn't try to hide her laugh this time. It did her heart good to see someone else set one of the Delgado men on his ear. They all thought they'd get their way if they just smiled. It was clear Martha cared for Ram, and yet she gave as good as she got.

The spirited nurse left after fussing with Ram's pillows, and Hallie couldn't resist teasing him. He grew red and protested so much she deduced a romance must be developing. Hallie couldn't help wondering how it would suit the younger Delgados to acquire a stepmother at this late date. A possibility, judging by Martha's attention and by the lovesick look in Ram's eyes. Hallie didn't think the sons would find this lady so easy to run off.

At last she took pity on Ram, stopped teasing him and set up the new chess set for a game. On the fifth move she captured his queen. On the eighth she had him in checkmate.

Sick or not, Ram Delgado did not like losing. He demanded a rematch. And so it went, until they were well into their third game, which he claimed to be winning. Suddenly he blurted, "Chino didn't do it, you know."

Hallie looked up from an intricate move, her brow furrowed. "Didn't do what?" she asked mildly.

"Didn't drain your gas tanks. Didn't have anyone do it, either."

Hallie's jaw dropped. "I thought you said Ivy was close-mouthed."

"Wasn't Ivy told me. Kirby stopped on his way to San Antone."

"I don't want to discuss it."

"Just like a woman. Hide your head in the sand."

"Oh? And I suppose you'll say Chino didn't paste a thousand chili-pepper stickers all over my trailer last night, too," she flared. "Or large Viva Terlingua banners—even though he made a big deal of spouting that silly phrase as he stomped out yesterday. Don't tell *me* what a nice guy he is."

" 'Viva Terlingua' is kind of the war cry of the big cook-off. The final-round judges taste an entry, drink a shot of tequila and everyone shouts, 'Viva Terlingua!' Sort of adds to the hype, if you know what I mean."

"Yes. Well, I don't like it hyped all over my tent-trailer, thank you very much. It'll take me weeks to peel them off."

"Don't know anything about any stickers. I'll grant you Chino's been a little wild in his time. All the boys acted out after their mother died. Hell, I did, too. Took a few years, but we all settled down."

"Really? You couldn't prove it by me."

The old man's jaw tensed. "Not one of my boys mistreats women. Their mother taught them respect. Respect and gentleness." His voice thinned. "Something they wouldn't have learned from a tough old duck like me."

Hallie glanced up and saw a distinct glistening at the corners of his eyes. "I don't know about that," she murmured softly. "You're the fortress. The patriarch. They all love you, Ram."

"You gonna take all day makin' that move, girl?"

"Uh, no." She pretended to study the board at length, allowing him time to compose himself. She didn't even scold him for calling her "girl." But her magnanimity didn't extend to letting him win. Hallie moved one piece and brought him into check. Checkmate, actually.

He blinked twice, then glared at her. "You musta swiped one of my pieces while I was blowing my damn nose."

She met his charge head-on. "You left yourself wide open. It was that last move. You shouldn't have made it."

"You cheated."

"I do not cheat."

He sank back against the pillows, crossed his arms and sulked.

Hallie noted lines of strain around his mouth and eyes. Enough had been said. Quietly she began gathering the chess pieces.

"I guess you didn't cheat," he admitted in a gravelly voice. "I'm gettin' old. Can't keep my mind on the game. I'm gonna rot here and no one's gonna give a damn."

"You had a rough setback, Ram. I shouldn't have come. Maybe it's too soon for company."

He reached for her hand. She felt the slight tremor, set the chess case aside and lifted her other hand to cover his. "I'll call late next week, and if you're up to it we'll try one game. I don't believe for a minute that there's anything wrong with your mind. You're sharp as a tack."

Ram's dark eyes gleamed and his fingers tightened around hers. "So then," he pounced, "you're willing to admit maybe I know what I'm talkin' about when I say my son isn't the one harassing you?"

Hallie didn't want to debate him. She tried pulling away, but his grip was too strong. She simply shook her head. If only he knew how desperately she wanted to believe Chino was innocent. With all her heart she wanted to lay blame elsewhere—but she'd heard those men with her own ears. "I won't argue, Ram. It won't help you get well."

He released her hand and punched the button to lower his bed. "Go then, since you don't trust a man on his death-bed to tell the truth. That boy is crazy about you. You're just too damned hardheaded to see."

Hallie stood and closed the lid on the chess case. "Deathbed? You wouldn't be trying to con me, would you?"

He stuck out a stubbled jaw and glowered.

Hallie sighed. He looked exhausted. And she was tired, too.

Suddenly the door squeaked open and in walked Chino and Ivy, talking and laughing. Both stopped the moment they saw Ram and Hallie squared off.

"What's going on?" Chino sauntered across to the bed.

Hallie watched the effortless swagger and instantly her hackles rose. Because, although Chino had asked the question of the room at large, his eyes were coldly drilling *her*. It was clear who he blamed for his father's upset.

"I was just leaving," she said, picking up her shoulder bag.

Chino turned to Ivy. "Thought Jesse said not to open up Dad's visitations. We have enough trouble without begging for more."

"Now just a darn minute." Hallie stopped short of Ram's bed.

"No, you wait," Chino began.

His father said, "Hush, both of you."

"Dad's lucky you don't have a frying pan," Chino said snidely, trapping Hallie between Ram's bed and the dresser. "What in hell were you fighting about?"

"What else?" she snapped. "You."

"Me? That's rich. What's your beef this time? There hasn't been another cook-off."

Ivy hurried over and placed a restraining hand on Chino's arm. "You're shouting, Chino. Surely there's no need to yell at Hallie like that."

"I'm not yelling." But he was, and Chino knew it. Hallie had that effect on him. He yanked off his Stetson, threw it on the bed and ran a hand through his hair. "I'm sorry," he said. "But Kirby already burdened Dad with all this, even after I said the old man'd chew it to death. Frankly, who knows whether your dammed gas tanks were full in the first place? I only have your word."

Hallie's eyes blazed. "My word? Just where were you last night during the witching hour, Mr. Sweetness and Light?"

"I don't know exactly what the witching hour is. But somehow I'm not surprised to hear that you do."

Hallie drew a sharp breath. "It's always word games with you, isn't it, Chino? You never answer a question straight. Well, I'm not buying it this time. You and those brush-faced, cretinous friends of yours decorated my trailer with bright red chili-pepper stickers last night—and don't think I don't know it.''

"What?" He caught her wrist, throwing her off balance.

She twisted her arm, breaking his hold. "I've decided to keep them. As a symbolic touch. To remind me what infantile tricks I can expect from you." Hallie settled the strap of her bag firmly on her shoulder, shot Ram a faint smile and marched to the door. Opening it, she turned and announced, "To repeat a clever phrase I heard yesterday, Viva Terlingua, Chino."

He stood with hands on hips, looking dumbfounded as she disappeared.

"You didn't do that—did you, son?" Ram asked wearily.

"Do what?" Chino massaged the back of his neck. "I feel as if I walked out on a stage in the middle of a three-act play without knowing my part. Ivy, do you have a clue what's going on?"

She shook her head.

"Good," Chino snorted, "because I don't either. Dad?"

Ram relayed a much-condensed version.

Chino paced as he listened. He stopped and stared out the window overlooking the parking lot. Hallie was striding through rows of cars, her hair ruffled by the wind. His breath stalled in his lungs. She looked so small. So defenseless. He angled the miniblinds for a better view. A crushing weight of regret and longing ripped through his heart. "I swear to you, Dad, I'm as much in the dark about these things that keep happening to her as she is. But I know this—it's gone way beyond a joke."

Ivy took the seat Hallie had vacated. "Don't you mean things happening to you both? If you ask me, someone's going to great lengths to make it look as if you're the culprit."

"And doing a damn good job of it," Chino agreed, snapping the blinds closed. "Those calls she's getting at night are plain harassment. And how long, I wonder, before one of those clowns crosses the line?"

"Sounds like a job for a white knight," Ivy said, winking at Ram. Chino glared.

"Yes, indeed." Ram nodded. "So what are you going to do, son?"

"Me?" Chino buried his hands in his back pockets.

"Now, Ram—" Ivy sounded bored with the subject "—why would Chino care what happens to Hallie? After all, they're opponents."

"I do care." Chino's voice rose. "And you both damn well know it. So help me, if any of it's your doing, to effect a little matchmaking or—"

"It's not," they said together as he grabbed his hat and stalked out.

"Go get 'em, tiger," Ivy cheered.

The elder Delgado flinched, then closed his eyes and smiled.

CHAPTER SEVEN

TUESDAY, Hallie had an unexpected visit from the Cedarville police. She was just coming in from the garden when Steve Hardin parked his cruiser beside her back door. Steve had been one of the first students she'd taught. The man in crisp khaki had come a long way from the heavy-metal rocker who delighted in bedeviling a new teacher. Hallie smiled. They'd both come a long way.

"Hi, Steve," she called. "Haven't seen you in ages. To what do I owe the pleasure?" Remembering her speeding ticket, she added, "I already stopped by the county clerk's office and paid my fine."

He pulled out a notebook. "I don't know anything about a fine. Mr. Delgado asked us to check out some vandalism you had. And I'm supposed to dig a little deeper into crank phone calls."

"That was sweet of Ram."

The young policeman glanced up. "Chino, the chief said."

"Chino?" Hallie laughed. "That's like the fox checking out the henhouse." She pointed to the stickers. "His handiwork, I believe."

"Don't think so, Ms. Bergstrom. Chief Potts said it sounds like a harmless prank, but Delgado insisted we take it seriously."

"Really?" Hallie was taken aback.

"Yes. Do you have anything to add to the report you filed?" Hardin asked, pulling out a pen and flipping the page. "The chief told me to ask if you ever called the phone company to report this man's calls."

"Actually I did, or at least I tried. By the time they transferred me to the fifth person, I began to think it sounded hokey myself. So I gave up and chalked it up to the cook-off thing. The first calls came after Penny Beth's story. But I don't know for certain it's a man. It could be a woman."

"Or a student," he pointed out. "You fail anybody in June?"

Hallie glanced up sharply. "I never considered my students."

"Why don't you list anybody you think might be holding a grudge? I'll go see if I can lift any prints."

Hallie took the piece of paper he offered and sat on her back steps. She'd been positive it was Chino's doing. Yet he'd gone to the police on her behalf, so... Hallie crumpled the paper. Forced now to face facts, she realized that all along it had just been too convenient to blame Chino. Why? Because she was desperate for any reason to keep him at arm's length? Or at least beyond kissing distance. But now what?

"I helped myself to a couple of your stickers," Steve said, rejoining her. "The lab may pick up something. The chief said to tell you we'll have to send this out. To Dallas, and they're slow."

"I just thought it was Chino or one of his buddies being cute. I honestly can't think of a single enemy."

His eyes twinkled. "I could name one. My mom. Dad plays darts three nights a week at the Cellar, and she'd love to see Chino turn it into a family restaurant—even if it isn't one of his chili chain."

"Invite your mother to join our literary club. We meet at the Cellar."

He said he would and handed her a business card. "Keep in touch. Call if anything else happens, or if the caller starts making threats."

Not liking his final remark, Hallie shivered. Darn it all, why was she such a wimp? Gram would have been on top of this mess herself. Hallie could almost hear her lecture—

Hallie, my girl, a person should get a spade and dig for solutions, not sit back waiting for answers to turn up. Unfortunately Hallie wasn't Gram. Truth was, she didn't know where to begin.

Call Chino and apologize, for starters, an inner voice nudged.

But when Hallie tried, her call netted Babs Delgado, Jesse's wife, and about all she learned was that Chino wasn't at the ranch. Nor was he expected anytime soon, according to Babs.

Hallie decided it was a good time to pick the last of Gram's special berries—the secret ingredient she was counting on to help her beat Chino. As she washed and prepared them for the freezer, Hallie wondered if they'd have the same flavor frozen. But really, she had no choice. It was the safest way to keep Chino from finding out what she used.

As it turned out, she needn't have worried. On her next visit to Ram, she learned that Chino had gone back to San Antonio.

"He told me Kirby's getting behind in the office," Ram said. "Between you, me and the gatepost, I think he's dodging Serita. What did you need him for?"

"I don't *need* him," Hallie murmured. "I sort of owe him an apology." But Ram's statement momentarily distracted her. Was it coincidence that the calls stopped while Chino was out of town? Maybe she *didn't* owe him an apology.

Hallie made a bad move with her queen, which gave Ram an easy victory.

"If he's got you so hot and bothered you make a mistake like that," Ram grumbled, "you should call him."

Hallie glared. "I can whip you with one hand tied behind my back, Ram Delgado. Set 'em up again."

Gleefully he obliged, and as he did, he also cross-examined her about her true feelings for Chino.

She got so flustered she lost two matches in a row.

Smug, Ram taunted her about calling his son. "Use my dime," he offered, smiling like a cat with a saucer of cream.

Fortunately, before Hallie dumped the chess pieces over his head, Martha brought his lunch. Ram's sudden transference of interest to his pretty nurse gave Hallie the perfect excuse to leave.

If by next week she still thought Chino deserved an apology, she'd call after her shopping trip to San Antonio with Glynnis and Evie. They were going to look for a wedding gown and bridesmaid dresses. Deciding whether or not he deserved an apology was giving Hallie fits. It did seem terribly coincidental that the calls stopped when he was gone. On the other hand, why would he go to the police if he was making them?

Ultimately Hallie chose to wait. Meanwhile, she sent in her application to cook at Luckenbach—an event that, luckily enough, fell on the weekend following Glynnis and Joe's wedding.

Evie promised to go with her to the women's cook-off, and Hallie's spirits picked up again. The week sped by. Hallie's phone remained quiet. So maybe Chino had duped her *and* the police. He was certainly capable of it, the charming rascal. Hallie made up her mind that hell would freeze over before she'd contact him now.

Around midnight the telephone beside Hallie's bed shrilled. A low, rasping voice garbled something about skipping San Antonio, then disconnected.

She struggled to sit up as the line went dead. Hallie's heart seemed to hammer up in her throat. Nothing about the call made sense. She would have understood being warned away from Luckenbach, but not a simple shopping trip with friends.

She switched on a lamp and realized she was still clutching the phone. Her hand shook as she replaced it. For no reason, she hopped out of bed and got the bear Chino had given her. Once again she found his soft bulk comforting.

Keyed up, she lay there, unable to sleep, for some time. But when the alarm sounded at dawn and she awoke with her arms wrapped around the stuffed animal, Hallie wondered if it had all been a bad dream.

By the time she finished her shower, she almost believed it had. If not the call, at least the warning. After all, it was paranoid to think anyone cared that she was going to San Antonio.

Because Evie owned an economy automobile, she'd been designated the driver today. At six on the dot, she and Glynnis arrived at Hallie's as planned.

"I didn't sleep a wink last night," Glynnis confided by way of greeting after Hallie had climbed into the back seat. "Guess I still can't believe it's me shopping for a wedding dress. Pinch me, Hallie, to see if this is real."

Hallie shook her head and laughed, but Evie promptly obliged.

"Ouch!" Glynnis rubbed her arm. "That hurt."

"So now you know it's real," Evie said, backing down the long driveway.

"Well, it's a darned good thing I'm going to look at long-sleeved dresses," Glynnis grumbled. "My arm will be black-and-blue for a month."

Evie grinned. "Does Joe know how you stretch the truth? If not, I think I'll tell him at breakfast."

"Breakfast?" Hallie threw Evie a glance. "What's Joe doing in San Antonio? Glynnis, don't you know it's bad luck for the groom to see the gown before the wedding?"

Glynnis adjusted her seat belt so she could turn around. "Chino invited him. Actually, he's asked Joe to manage one of his Chili Houses in Dallas. It's more money and better hours. His orientation is in San Antonio this week. We decided it was a good opportunity to pick out our wedding bands, as well. But don't fret, Chino said you and Evie can stay at his house while we're out."

"Uh, Hallie...Chino's having a small get-together tonight. Kind of a combination welcome-to-the-company and engagement party."

"Why didn't you tell me any of this sooner? Besides—" Hallie brushed a hand over her denim dress "—I'm not dressed for a party." Her tone said she was hurt.

Glynnis flushed, averting her gaze.

Evie piped up again, "Frankly, we were afraid you wouldn't go. And you look fine. You always look like you stepped out of a fashion magazine." She caught Hallie's eye in the mirror. "See, your scarf and belt are exactly the same shade of red as your boots."

But Hallie's mind had skipped beyond accessories. It was on her night caller's gravelly warning. "Who all has Chino invited?" she asked abruptly.

"I don't have any idea," Glynnis said. "Presumably people Joe will deal with at work. Why?"

"No reason," Hallie mumbled. She wished she'd listened harder to the caller's voice. She'd been awfully quick to rule Chino out. Maybe too quick...

Soon their talk drifted to Glynnis's wedding and the dresses.

"I hope you choose something Hallie and I can wear *after* the wedding," Evie said. "Why is it that bridesmaid dresses are so distinctive? I have a closetful from my sisters' weddings. If Hallie wasn't so skinny, we could've each picked one of those and saved some money."

"Money's tight for everyone," Glynnis agreed. "I'd like a sundress in pastel with maybe a tiny lavender flower. In a style you can wear again."

"What a great idea, Glynnis." Hallie squeezed her friend's shoulder. "Frankly, it won't matter what Evie and I wear. All eyes will be on you."

"Just as well," Evie muttered good-naturedly. "I wouldn't want anyone to notice I'm green with envy." She turned and winked at Hallie. "You and I should make a pact—have a double wedding or stay old maids forever."

Hallie laughed. "Old we're not. And forever is a long time. I'll remind you of this conversation when you're the radiant bride. Remember what Gram said—if you want to find true love, you have to stop looking."

"Will you two quit bickering?" Glynnis begged. "Hey—" she nudged Evie's arm "—there's the restaurant. And there's Joe and Chino. Oh, they've got a third man to even the numbers."

Evie swiveled her head. "Oh, you mean the bald fat guy?"

Glynnis twisted around to peer more closely. "No. He's waiting for the streetlight to change. I meant the good-looking one just behind Joe. Over there." She pointed. "But even if the guy *was* bald, you shouldn't be so judgmental, Evie. Another of Hallie's Gram-isms went something like, if the grass looks greener on the other side of the fence, then it's time to fertilize."

"Hallie's Gram was a real Pollyanna. And between you two, it's getting hip-boot deep in here. Help me find a parking space. I'll go check out this paragon. If it turns out the good-looking one is waiting for his wife, I'll never let you hear the end of it."

He wasn't. Chino introduced his friend as Daniel O'Malley, old college classmate and owner of a marketing firm in San Antonio.

Hallie knew from Dan's humorous opening lines that he and Evie were well matched. Both had a dry wit and ready laughter. Chino, however, seemed unusually reserved. At least with her, for he joked with the others. Hallie experienced a little of that jealousy Evie had mentioned. But maybe "jealous" wasn't precisely the right term. Certainly she felt uncomfortable.

Their party of six was seated at a large round table. A waiter had poured coffee and handed breakfast menus all around before Chino finally directed a comment Hallie's way.

"Dad called me yesterday," he began. "He said you wanted to talk to me. It was after midnight when I left work or I would've phoned you."

Hallie pretended to study the menu. Her heart thumped hard against her ribs. "Or maybe you did call," she said off-handedly.

Chino's brows rose. "I just said I didn't, Hallie. That means I didn't." He paused to draw a deep breath. "Is that jerk up to his tricks again?"

"Again?" Hallie impaled him with her eyes. "How did you know the calls had stopped?"

Chino's dark gaze concealed nothing. "I visited the police. I know Steve Hardin followed up. Give it to me straight, Hallie. No games."

She pushed a lock of hair out of her eyes. "All right. For over a week, I didn't have any calls. Last night, late, someone rang and more or less suggested I stay home today. My point is—who knew about this trip?"

Chino's breath hissed through his teeth loudly enough to halt the others' conversation. "Damn it, Hallie. Why didn't you phone the police? Or me?"

She was saved from answering by the waiter who'd come to take their orders. He left, and Chino pulled out a business card, wrote on it and tucked it under Hallie's hand. "My home and office numbers. Next time, don't wait!"

Hallie gazed at him for a moment, trying to decide if he was truly worried or if this was all show. Reading nothing but concern in his eyes, she nodded and slipped the card into her purse.

Chino fooled with his silverware. He didn't like the dark circles under Hallie's eyes or the wary look she'd given him. Mentally he reviewed tonight's guest list—mostly people from his corporate office. Friends he wanted Hallie and her friends to meet. Not a single cook-off buff. He figured a party would be a more relaxed way for everyone to get acquainted. But from the way Hallie was acting, he wished he hadn't bothered.

Their waiter returned carrying a tray of sparkling juice and water for everyone. He leaned between Evie and Daniel to place the first glass, and for some crazy reason the tray tipped.

Chino shouted a warning.

Dan bolted from his chair and sent the whole tray crashing to the floor. Glasses flew. Evie suffered the brunt of the dousing. A quick move on Daniel's part saved her from being hit by a heavy glass.

The waiter was horrified, but Evie sought to reassure him. "It's okay. One of those things." She laughed and pulled her drenched blouse away from her skin. "Glynnis said I needed to mend my ways. Do you suppose this is an omen?"

The manager rushed up and offered to send Evie's clothes out for cleaning. Daniel supplied a more immediate solution. "My sister lives a few blocks away. You and she are about the same size, I'd guess. I'll run you over there and you can borrow something to wear while you shop." He took off his suit jacket and placed it around Evie's shoulders.

She smiled her thanks, sending a helpless shrug toward Glynnis.

"Sounds like the best plan," the bride-to-be admitted.

Joe picked up her hand and said, "We could look for wedding bands first. You ladies can do dresses later."

Glynnis made a face. "I hope this isn't indicative of things to come."

"Seems like good luck—for me, anyway," Dan joked, guiding Evie between tables.

Chino trailed them for a few steps. "Come to my house after you see to Evie's needs," he told Dan. "We'll all touch base there."

Dan agreed, and the others were moved to a new table where they ate without much talk. When they'd finished and Glynnis and Joe got up to go, it struck Hallie that circumstances would leave her alone with Chino.

"Why don't I take a cab to one of the malls and meet you later?" she suggested to Glynnis.

"I thought you wanted to see my house?" Chino glanced up from where he was critically perusing a check that had been zeroed out.

Hallie bit her lip, saying nothing.

Glynnis seemed torn between going and staying, and Hallie felt guilty. "You're right, Chino. I did say that." What else could she do? Enough had already gone wrong for Glynnis.

She peered over Chino's shoulder at the check. "I don't feel right about their not charging us for breakfast, Chino. The waiter feels terrible as it is."

"Exactly." Chino shook Joe's hand. "I'll take care of this. You two go find those gold bands." He dropped bills for a tip, took the check and asked Hallie to wait in the foyer.

Twice she assured Glynnis that the arrangements were fine, even though she wasn't fully convinced herself. Stoically, she sent them off with a cheerful wave.

"It's a good thing Dan brought his car," Chino said casually on his return. "Hey, don't scowl like that." He brushed a finger across her knotted brow. "They say that if things go wrong before a wedding, the ceremony will be smooth." He escorted her to the door, his hand light against her back.

Hallie warmed to his mood and the heat of his touch. "It was sort of funny, you know," she said. "The scene would be hysterical in a movie. Come to think of it, we must have looked a lot like Laurel and Hardy—all of us jumping around, snatching up napkins, rolling up the tablecloth."

"Yeah." He laughed. "Now that you mention it, I do recall the restaurant sure got quiet in a hurry." Unlocking the passenger door of a blue, low-slung sports car sandwiched between two trucks, he motioned for her to get in.

"Wow," Hallie exclaimed. "Where's your truck?"

"I use this in town."

She sank into the soft leather upholstery, and for the first time, really took note of what Chino was wearing today. A double-breasted navy gabardine suit with a silk print tie. Gone were the ever-present cowboy boots and the snug, Western-cut jeans. Hallie wasn't sure how she felt about that and retreated into silence. Chino's new look would take some getting used to.

He didn't notice she'd gone quiet. Effortless as a tour guide, he pointed out landmarks as he expertly negotiated the heavy morning traffic.

Almost before Hallie had settled back to enjoy the trip, it ended. He turned into a circular brick driveway outside a beautiful, old Spanish-style home. "Wow! The pictures didn't do this justice," she breathed.

"Glad you like it." He parked and hurried around the car, smiling as he leaned inside to assist her out of the low bucket seat. "It was pretty run-down. I could hardly believe my luck in picking it up for back taxes."

Preoccupied with identifying the elusive scent of his cologne, Hallie missed what he said about restoration. She was not prepared to step through the carved double doors into the home of her dreams. Polished wood floors, white stucco alcoves lit by skylights, a sunken living room done in deep-piled, earth-tone carpets. She'd planned this interior a thousand times.

Blindly Hallie followed Chino through to a roomy kitchen made more spacious by a gleaming Spanish-tiled floor. Because he seemed to be waiting for some sort of response, she blurted out the first thing that came into her head. "Goodness, Chino, you must employ a platoon of maids."

He laughed and opened a door leading out to a pool and a tiered patio. "I'd like to say no and impress you, but with five thousand feet of living space, five acres of landscaped grounds and me gone a lot..."

She stepped out and leaned over a wrought-iron railing. Her gaze swept a row of stately oaks shading the sloped hillside. "I'm surprised Serita was willing to leave all this," she muttered, not realizing she'd spoken aloud.

Chino frowned. "Serita was long gone before I bought this house. She's never set foot inside. Not that she wouldn't like to. Actually, Hallie, *you* had more influence on how the place turned out."

"Me?"

He grasped her arm. "Don't tell me you don't remember our walk in the foothills the night you gave me a bottle of Grey Flannel cologne for my eighteenth birthday. We ended up on that rise overlooking Ben Molina's hacienda. You gave me a twenty-minute, room-by-room discourse on the way you'd decorate that house."

The corners of her mouth lifted. "Oh, I remember. And you spent the whole twenty minutes trying to unbutton my blouse."

His fingers tightened on her arm. His thick dark eyelashes dropped, hiding something. Contrition, perhaps? Or amusement?

"Yeah," he murmured. "First time my technique ever failed. But the picture you painted of those damned rooms was indelibly stamped on my brain."

"Really?" Hallie licked a suddenly dry bottom lip and returned to the kitchen, wishing he wasn't still wearing the scent she had selected then.

He came up behind her, lightly running the tips of his fingers from her elbows up over her shoulders. "The blouse was yellow with sprigs of white daisies. Your skin tasted like honey from the comb."

Feeling a shiver creep up her spine, Hallie gravitated toward the warmth radiating through his white shirt. "Chino—"

He turned her to face him and the kiss caught them both by surprise. His lips, though soft, devoured hers with long-leashed hunger.

Her guard dropped in the face of old memories. She received his kiss and matched it with a passion too long denied.

Time passed unnoticed as Chino took the kiss deeper and Hallie strained against him. She accepted the dark flavors of his tongue, listening to the shiver of need that shot through her.

Years before Chino might have failed, but this time the buttons on her blouse seemed to melt through the holes until his fingers rested on the front clasp of her bra. He was a whisper away from parting it when an embarrassed cough and someone's indrawn breath catapulted them back to reality.

First to recover, Chino thrust Hallie behind him. He gaped at a trio of middle-aged women. Then something clicked. Damn. He'd forgotten all about the caterers he'd hired to prepare Glynnis and Joe's party.

"Ah...you gave us a key, Mr. Delgado," the woman with the pinkest cheeks offered by way of explanation.

"Yes." Another, who could well have been her twin, bobbed her head. "We agreed on eleven o'clock." She whipped out a contract bearing Chino's signature.

He ran an unsteady hand around the back of his neck. "Do you have things to bring in from your van? Could you give us a minute, please?"

The women seemed relieved at the chance to escape.

He turned to Hallie, who was doing up her buttons with fumbling fingers. "Here, let me. You've got it crooked."

"What must those women think?" she hissed.

"Why should they think anything? This is *my* home."

"Yes, well, it's not mine." She pushed him away and tried to straighten her scarf, then combed nervous fingers through her hair. "You may do this sort of thing frequently, but I'm not accustomed to having strangers see...having them watch..." She turned away, making a frustrated noise in her throat.

"I don't do this frequently," he said in a calm voice. "But it felt damn good. And I'm not going to apologize. You enjoyed it well enough yourself, I might add, so don't be going all self-righteous."

She glared at him, hands on hips. "In all of these five thousand square feet do you happen to have a powder room?"

"Down the hall to the right, or up the stairs and left. Instead of running away, Hallie, don't you think this time we need to talk?" She did run, though, as fast as her legs would carry her.

"At least tell me why I can't seem to keep my hands off you," he called. "Tell me why, since the day we met, I have no control around you."

Hallie stopped when she reached the staircase. Her eyes blazed. "Oh, I think you managed quite well—once." Leaving him, she stumbled up the stairs and searched out the bathroom. Knees weak from the encounter and the climb, she bolted the door. She didn't know how long she stayed there. After some time she heard the doorbell chime. Only Dan's deep voice and Evie's laughter coaxed her out.

Even then she avoided looking at Chino and was much relieved when Glynnis and Joe showed up and everyone's attention was focused on the new wedding bands. At the first opportunity, Hallie suggested they go look for dresses, never trusting herself to meet Chino's gaze.

On the way to the car she thought of pleading ill so she could miss the party. She couldn't imagine why he'd made that outrageous statement about his lack of control, considering she'd thrown herself at him in that hayloft and he had walked out. She knew her nerves weren't strong enough to handle another romantic interlude; they never had been.

"The jeweler gave me the names of several bridal shops," Glynnis said once they were all buckled in. "Where shall we start?"

Evie named a shop Dan's sister had recommended. "Of course, it may be out of our price range. She lives in a pretty posh area. What do you think, Hallie? Do you feel flush?"

Hallie automatically put a hand to her cheek.

"Hallie?" Glynnis glanced over her shoulder. "Did you and Chino have another fight? You've hardly spoken since Joe and I got back."

"Uh . . . we didn't fight . . . exactly."

"Why don't you cut the man some slack?" Evie demanded. "Daniel said Chino's been in a lather all week, wanting everything to be right for you."

"Why would he say that? The party's for Joe and Glynnis."

Evie pursed her lips. "Hallie, sometimes for a teacher you're awfully dense. Try noticing how Chino looks at you."

"There!" Glynnis broke into the gathering argument, a lilt to her voice. "The bridal boutique—across the street. Omigosh, I've got cold feet all of a sudden."

Somehow her admission brought the release of tension they needed. Hallie and Evie stopped bickering and joined forces to shore up their waffling friend. Soon, *all* men were forgotten in a world filled with seed pearls, satin and lace.

They were so involved in searching for the perfect gowns, darkness fell without their being aware. All three were seated in velvet chairs at a shop where they'd been twice before, three pairs of high heels kicked every which way, when a clerk announced that Glynnis was wanted on the phone. They were shocked to hear the engagement party was already in full swing. Not only were they forced to stop dallying and choose, but Hallie suddenly realized she hadn't laid the groundwork to fake an illness.

In the end, she didn't even try. Glynnis was radiant in the gown she'd finally chosen. So much so that Hallie and Evie fell together blubbering like demented fools. They laughed and cried alternately all the way to Chino's house.

Contented, Hallie burrowed under bags and boxes in the back seat. If anyone had asked her to describe her mood, she'd probably say sentimental. Even if she'd truly been ill, she wouldn't have admitted it and missed one second of Glynnis's excitement.

As the trio joined the revelers, Hallie let her new emotions expand to include the party's host.

"You should have seen her, Chino," she said for about the third time. He'd introduced her to his friends, and now they shared a love seat in one of the secluded alcoves. "I've never seen Glynnis so...so..." She tested words like "radiant" and "dazzling," then discarded them for "pure."

Facing him, their knees nearly touching, Hallie placed her hand in his. Animated, she said, "I can't explain it, Chino. Glynnis just blossomed. There seemed to be this...this goodness radiating from within." She sighed contentedly.

It took all of Chino's willpower to sit and listen. If Hallie only knew how many times he'd thought the same of her.

How good she was. How pure. The night he'd wanted her so badly—after his high school graduation. That look she'd just described had nearly ripped out his heart. Leaving her untouched had been the hardest thing he'd ever done.

As her small hand warmed his larger one, Chino saw again that Hallie Bergstrom hadn't changed. Judging from the way he'd acted in the kitchen today, *he* had, but not for the better. Reliving old guilt, Chino shook off her fingers. He needed to establish some distance while his self-respect was still intact.

Hallie stopped midsentence as he stood and walked away. A sharp pain knifed through her heart. It was happening again. She should have known all his talk about being attracted to her had been a lie. A lie to let her think . . . well, never mind. It was obvious what he thought. Look how fast he ran. And he'd talked about *her* running away! The mystery was why she kept coming back.

Suddenly she recalled losing herself in his kisses—and she knew. She loved Chino Delgado, and nothing would ever change that.

The remainder of the evening was difficult for Hallie. Glynnis and Joe held hands. Evie was ensconced in a corner with Daniel O'Malley, talking up a storm. It seemed to Hallie there were nothing but happy couples everywhere.

When the time came to say goodbye and go back to Cedarville, only Hallie was happy to see the evening end.

The crowning blow came when Evie begged off going to the chili cook-off in Luckenbach because Daniel had invited her to his company picnic.

Hallie didn't cry then, even though she felt like it.

Neither of her friends seemed to notice her dejection during the ride home. They dropped her off and waited while she went into her dark house. Hallie's worst moment came as she returned the key to her purse and found the business card on which Chino had listed his phone numbers.

She tore it in two, and couldn't help wondering if Chino had been behind Daniel's convenient invitation. For Evie's sake, Hallie hoped not. But if he thought she would opt out of Luckenbach on that account, he was sadly mistaken.

She dropped the pieces of his card into the trash. If ever she could use a Gram-ism it was now, when she felt lower than a snake's belly.

Just then the telephone rang, and Hallie felt the tears she'd been holding back break loose and trickle down her cheeks.

CHAPTER EIGHT

HALLIE SHED her light wrap and stared at the ringing phone. It clicked to her answering machine. Suddenly there was a snap and a whir, and she realized the tape had broken. Hallie breathed a sigh of relief. Even at that, the call made her nervous. Her home was fairly remote. If she stood on tiptoe she could just see the McDermotts' porch light, which she did now so she wouldn't feel quite so alone.

The phone shrilled again. Sleep was out of the question. Not wanting to hear it ring, she yanked the plug from the wall. Tomorrow she might call the phone company again. Tonight, however, she would deal with her case of nerves the same way she had when Gram was so sick.

Marching into the kitchen, Hallie pulled out ingredients for chocolate chip cookies. A double batch. It felt good to be doing something physical. By and by, her mind gravitated to the pleasant aspects of today's trip. Glynnis would make a beautiful bride. She'd also be sorely missed at school and in the literary club. Sadly, Hallie thought how the club would change with Glynnis gone. And what about Evie? She seemed very interested in Daniel O'Malley. Suddenly, her plan to save the Cellar seemed pointless. Pointless and a bit depressing.

In spite of her rambling mind, Hallie's first batch of cookies was ready to bake. She had them in the oven and was beginning the next batch when the lights of a slow-moving vehicle flashed across her window. Her heart leapt and her mouth went dry as a creek bed in summer. She was searching for the phone jack when a soft knock sounded at her door. She panicked. The kitchen clock read 2 a.m.

"Hallie, damn it, open up. I can hear you in there."

Chino? She tiptoed to the door. Edging the curtain aside, she was shocked to see him silhouetted in the moonlight. Gone were his suit and tie. Back were the boots, his worn gray Stetson and hip-hugging jeans.

She undid the lock and opened the door just as a buzzer heralded completion of her first tray of cookies. Leaving him to fend for himself, she ran back across the room, slid an oven mitt on one hand and almost in a single motion removed the hot pan and replaced it with a second sheet neatly dotted with mounds of dough.

Chino closed the door and swept off his hat. "What in hell are you doing?" he asked, sending the hat sailing into one of the captain's chairs at her kitchen table. "Is there something wrong with your phone?"

With a calmness belying her recent scare, Hallie proceeded to unload the steaming cookies onto an aluminum rack. "Oh, I unplugged it."

"Hallie, I swear. Are you trying to drive me crazy?" He paced around the table, skirted the counter and came to stand beside her. Reaching an arm around her, he tested one of the hot cookies with a finger. "These smell great. May I?" He didn't wait for her answer and was forced to grab for falling bits as the cookie broke apart in his hand.

Hallie watched him carry a moist piece to his lips. She fought hard against a rush of heat prickling her spine. "The tape on my answering machine broke. I didn't want to deal with it tonight. What did you want?"

"To make sure you got home okay," he said. "The second time you didn't answer, I got worried. I called the ranch to see if Ivy would come check. Cody told me what I could do with that idea. He never did like being hauled out of the sack."

"Why on earth would you call to see if I made it home?" Hallie asked. "You barely managed a civil goodbye when I left."

Chino licked a sliver of chocolate from one finger, shrugged, then reached for a second cookie.

Hallie slapped his hand. "You were saying?"

He turned to her, instead, slipping his hands beneath her heavy fall of hair. He tipped her head back. His eyes were dark. Moody.

Suddenly nervous, Hallie grabbed two cooling cookies and shoved them into his shirtfront in a wordless offering.

His lips parted in a grin. "Hallie, Hallie," he said, dropping his hands and shaking his head as he accepted the cookies. "Do you have any coffee to go with these?"

"No, but it'll only take a minute to make some."

He nodded, helped himself to a napkin and set the cookies on the counter. While she made coffee, he peeked in the oven. The buzzer went off and he jumped, slamming the oven door shut. At Hallie's laugh, he grabbed a mitt and pulled out the pan, then unloaded the tray.

"Dad called me tonight," he said casually. "He's going home tomorrow."

Stepping around him with another tray, Hallie glanced up in surprise. "Why, Chino, that's wonderful news."

"He's taking a circuitous route—via the courthouse. To get married."

Her eyes widened. "Martha?"

"You knew?" Chino accused.

"No. But all the signs were there."

"Jesse and I think he's slipped a cog."

She filled two mugs with coffee. "She seems nice. I hope you guys don't try to run her off the way you did your housekeepers. After all, she won't be taking your mother's place. You're all adults now."

"Thank you for the five-minute, fifty-cent psychiatric evaluation," he said sarcastically.

"You want coffee and cookies or a fight?" The buzzer cut her off.

Chino let her handle the hot pan. This time he placed the new sheet on the middle rack and carefully shut the door. "I guess what I wanted was sympathy, but I can see whose side you're on."

"Give Martha a chance, Chino. She makes him laugh. He loves her."

"Love!" he snorted. "What would you know about love?"

"Nothing." Hallie folded her hands, still, they trembled. "Even a person who thinks he knows everything—like you, Chino—sometimes has room to learn. I think you'd better go," she said primly. "It's late and I'm tired."

Her words tore at his heart. Though his feet carried him around the table where he picked up his hat, Chino didn't want to leave. He wanted to take Hallie in his arms and show her what he knew about love. Hell, he wanted to love her until morning. Love her and be loved by her for a lifetime. But too much stood in their way. Old misunderstandings. New doubts. That damned chili cook-off. And now his dad's sudden marriage.

Chino tugged his hat down to his brows and flicked two fingers across the brim in a salute. "I'm off to San Marcos for the Chilympiad right after the old man's wedding," he said, catching her eye. "If you need anything while I'm gone, call Jesse. And lock this door when I leave. Wouldn't want somebody stealing the best damn chocolate chip cookies I've ever tasted." In two strides he circled the table, picked up his uneaten cookies and, without warning, leaned across the counter and gave her a quick, hard kiss.

Before Hallie recovered, his truck was rumbling down the driveway. She smiled and ran a finger softly over her lips as she double-locked the door.

So, Ram was getting married? Seemed there was a lot of that going around.

Hallie removed the pan of cookies Chino had put in the oven. The big phony. He was more like his father than he cared to admit. They were both like toasted marshmallows—all mush underneath a crusty shell.

But she was glad he planned to go to Ram's wedding. And...he'd worried about her. That was nice. Smiling, she bit into a warm cookie and savored the rich taste of chocolate. A man who liked chocolate chip cookies as much as she did couldn't be all bad. With a yawn, Hallie bundled the remaining dough to freeze for another day. Perhaps she could sleep, after all.

A WEEK LATER—a full week after Chino's visit—Hallie sat gazing at her fall calendar. She would've liked to attend Ram's wedding, but she understood the need to limit the service to family. She'd sent a gift to the ranch. Today there was a nice article in the late-summer events section of the *Cedarville Sentinel*. It was hard to believe summer was winding down, she mused, draining the double-mocha espresso Glynnis had brought her from the Cellar.

A snappy knock sounded on her back door, and she assumed it must be Glynnis on her return run. "It's unlocked," Hallie called. To her surprise, Penny Beth Frazier opened the door and popped her head inside.

"Hallie," she said a little stiffly, "my boss asked me to do a feature story on the secret ingredients some of you sneak into your chili. Would you be willing to discuss yours?"

Amused, Hallie leaned back in her chair. "You've got to be kidding."

"I'm not." Penny Beth paced. "Article's past due. No one'll talk."

"Did you honestly think they would? A story like that should cap the Terlingua cook-off. Only a fool would spill the beans before then." She laughed at her own joke.

Penny Beth didn't. "The feature editor wants it now. To be perfectly honest, Hallie, the man is an ogre. Can't you give me a little hint, something I can build a story around?"

"Did Chino send you?"

"No, but I've just come from the Chilympiad. I couldn't get a straight answer there, either. Those jokers listed things like rattlesnake meat, armadillo and bug juice. One old geezer said he used buzzard's breath, cigar ash and farkleberries. Not a single person took me seriously."

"So write a spoof. By the way," Hallie asked casually, "who won?"

"Hank took first. Some obnoxious creep from east Texas was second and Chino picked up third. Loco Louie, out of Bandera, tied for fourth with a college kid who was there on a dare."

Hallie mentally calculated—Chino still didn't have enough points. Only Hank qualified. Hallie didn't like Hank. He was the worm who'd gotten her into this mess. Sometimes the way he looked at her made her skin crawl.

She gave a start as she realized Penny Beth was talking again.

"Maybe I will take your suggestion and write a funny piece, Hallie. Oh, by the way, not to change the subject, but I was kind of surprised to see the announcement come in about your friend marrying Joe Bonner next Saturday."

"Why? They're a perfect couple."

Penny Beth inspected a fingernail. "Babs Delgado said you and your two friends sucked up to Chino to get Joe that job." She fluffed her blond curls.

Hallie battled a growing urge to toss her out on her ear.

"I hope that's all it was," Penny Beth continued. "Babs is going to help *me* land Chino. She's mad at Serita since she took up with Hank Edwards. Even though it was Babs's suggestion—just to make Chino jealous. Her plan backfired when Hank inherited his dad's feed store and a pile of cash. Honestly, Serita is so superficial." The reporter closed her notebook.

Hallie hated small-town gossip. But darn, this was interesting. If there was any truth to it... Hallie found herself walking Penny Beth to the door. "Hank Edwards and Serita? The Hank who won the Chilympiad, right?"

"Habanero Hank. That's him," Penny Beth acknowledged, taking care as she navigated Hallie's back steps in her spiky heels. "When he won yesterday, the stupid man drank a margarita from Serita's shoe. *She* carried on like an adolescent. If Serita thinks Chino was impressed, she's dead wrong. He wasn't in the least. Distaste was all I saw on his face."

Hallie stood in the doorway. No way would she comment and fuel this woman's tale. "Good luck with your article," she said, excusing herself to go back inside where she could piece together what she'd just learned.

And what exactly was that? Hallie wondered as she sat down to pay her bills. Babs and Penny Beth were suddenly thick as black crude in a new gusher. Chino's ex was playing footsie with a man bent on winning this year's cook-off. And Chino. Was it really distaste Penny Beth had observed?

More to the point, Hallie thought in disgust, why should she be wasting her time worrying about any of them? What she needed to do next was sort through her closet to see what needed replacing before school started. And that was supposing she had any money left.

To Hallie's delight, she discovered that she had more money than usual, although she found it hard to believe that attending cook-offs and buying a bridesmaid dress cost less than her normal summer activities. But there was no disputing what her bank statement said in black and white. And now she could afford to get Glynnis and Joe the crystal salad bowl she'd had her eye on at Bronson's, too.

She was heading out the door to do just that when the phone rang. "Yes?" Hallie said, snatching it up midring.

"Hallie, that you?" Ram Delgado asked.

"Well, well," she said, a teasing lilt to her voice. "How's married life treating you?"

"Been hell, darlin'." He chuckled, low and deep. Reminiscent of Chino's laugh, Hallie thought.

"It's like trying to honeymoon at Grand Central Station. But the doc won't let me leave town until after my next checkup, so I'm stuck until he does. Then I'm not tellin' one of these nosy kids where to find us."

"Ah, I see. Ram, you're welcome to use my house this weekend. I'm going to Dallas to a friend's wedding. Gram's bed is a four-poster that withstood thirty years of marriage."

"And just what do you know about things like that, young lady?"

"I...um...I..." Hallie was caught totally off guard.

"Damned if Chino's manners aren't improving—and so's his taste in women. I may just take you up on that offer, darlin', long as you zip your lip around Ivy and Chino. And don't let a horny old buzzard like me embarrass you. I'll be less testy after a weekend alone with my wife. Why, a man can't even go to the bathroom here without someone interrupts. Plus...the damn bed squeaks."

It was Hallie's turn to laugh. "Mum's the word. How about if I leave a key under the back doormat? I'm heading out Friday morning."

"Darlin', I thank you, and Martha thanks you."

"Why did you call, Ram? I'm sure it wasn't to book a honeymoon suite."

"Damn, I almost forgot. Come here tonight. Barbecue at eight o'clock.

"Well?" he demanded, when she didn't respond.

"Whose idea was it?" she asked.

"Mine. I'm still top dog out here, you know?"

"Fine. Thanks. What can I bring?"

"Bottle of sangria and a carton of cigarettes. I'll meet you by the big live oak out front, five to eight."

"There's a limit to my aiding and abetting. No dice. Those are both taboo for a recovering heart patient."

"I take back all the nice things I said about you." He sighed. "Bring yourself, lass. Wheat's harvested. There's enough food to feed half the county."

Hallie said goodbye and then left to do her errands. She wondered what Babs and Jesse would say when she waltzed in. Ram might think he was top dog, but those two had been running the ranch ever since he'd gotten sick. Hallie sincerely doubted her evening would be dull.

Dull might have been preferable, she reflected, shortly after arriving at the Delgado ranch. Ram, the sneak, hadn't said it was a family party, except for her. In a tense moment, when Babs demanded to know who had invited her and Ram roared like an injured bear, Hallie wanted to strangle him for having implied half the county was invited.

She found herself sticking close to Martha, who managed to smile and be gracious in spite of the daggers Babs aimed her way. The third generation of Delgados, Babs and Jesse's children, splashed her from the pool, the same as they did Ivy. Tension eased a bit after Ram ladled out large glasses of homemade sangria, excluding himself, and Martha brought in deep crocks of chili con queso and spicy bean dip.

Hallie had a giant corn chip laden with the gooey mixture halfway to her mouth when Chino sauntered in with Kirby and Louisa. Mumbling a garbled hello, Hallie was mortified when the chip broke and cheese dribbled between her fingers, and all eyes turned her way. It was a miracle how quickly Chino unloaded the case of Lone Star beer he'd brought and came to her rescue. He caught the chip and its mess of cheese and dip, too—except for one drop on her jade silk blouse.

Chino whipped out his handkerchief and scrubbed at the spot above the tip of her left breast. She gazed at him helplessly as suddenly her nipple hardened and the air between them sizzled.

He felt her stiffen. "Did it burn you, Hallie?"

She swallowed and shook her head, knowing it was her face that was on fire. She glanced around to see who might have observed the spark of desire before she'd banked it. Ivy suppressed a knowing smile, but continued to munch on chips. Ram smirked openly and gave her a thumbs-up. Hallie almost choked. She was saved when Cody announced the brisket was done.

From then on everyone bantered—the type of good-natured rivalry common in large families, especially among competitive males. As one funny story after another unfolded, Hallie couldn't remember ever having laughed so hard. If a prank or challenge existed, one of the Delgado men had tried it.

"Your poor mother," Martha said during a lull, after the regaling of a particularly harrowing escapade. "She must have been gray before her time."

Jesse stood suddenly and the laughter died away. "Mother was *always* beautiful. That picture over the fireplace—the one you told Babs to remove—is the way she looked up to the day she died."

"But I didn't..." Martha began. Her words trailed off as Babs scrambled to her feet and began gathering plates. The new Mrs. Delgado sent Ram a look, then closed her mouth. But the mood was broken. Martha scraped back her chair and dashed from the room. Ram glared at his eldest son who had just wrenched the cap off a warm beer. Mutinous, Ram followed his wife out.

Ivy slammed down her fork. "Good show, Jesse. Real mature."

Babs flew to his defense. "Leave Jesse alone. Ram had no right moving that woman in here."

"Just hold it, everyone," Chino demanded. "Dad cleared this land and built this house. It's his to do with as he wants."

"He built it for our mother," Jesse snapped.

Louisa reached for Kirby's hand. She was clearly uncomfortable.

Cody threw down his napkin and stood. "Why don't you ladies go into the living room. Take the kids. This battle's been brewing for weeks. We need to hash it out."

"I think I'll just leave," Hallie murmured. "Ivy, please thank Ram for inviting me. Tell him I'll call later."

"Wait." Chino put a hand on her arm. "I'd like your help picking out a wedding gift for Joe and Glynnis. And will you ride with me to the service?"

"All the way to Dallas?" Babs gasped.

Chino looked mildly surprised. "What's the problem, Babs?"

"Penny Beth is doing a story on the wedding. She didn't want to go alone. I said she could probably go with you."

"Well, she can't. Damn it, Babs—"

Jesse stepped between them. "Hold it, little brother. Don't take that tone with my wife."

Hallie felt Chino's fingers tighten on her wrist. She didn't want to cause more problems. "I'm leaving, Chino. And I'm riding to the wedding with Evie." She disengaged her arm and retrieved her purse.

"No." He detained her. "Daniel's taking Evie." Dogging her footsteps, he bumped into his father in the hall. Chino sidestepped, ignoring Ram.

But an angry Ram Delgado wasn't a man to ignore. "Stay, Hallie, or go if you'd rather." His tone was brusque. "My family's about to have a long overdue discussion on who's captain of this ship."

"I'll call you later," Chino promised as Hallie opened the door. "Don't make any plans for the wedding until you hear from me." He stalled her again. "This time, answer your damn phone."

"Phew," she muttered as the door banged shut. "I hope they don't all go down with the ship."

SHORTLY AFTER MIDNIGHT, Hallie's phone rang. She was in bed reading and put the book aside to eye the instrument with some trepidation. Was it Chino, or was it her crank caller, who'd given her a few nights' reprieve? "Hello," she said, a bit breathless.

"Did I wake you?" Chino sounded weary.

"No. I was reading. Is everything okay with you? I was proud of you for sticking up for Martha. You weren't keen on their getting married."

"It's his home. But Jesse and Dad are a lot alike. Truth is, Jess has a lot more invested in the ranch than any of the rest of us."

"But you're right. It *is* your father's house."

"He's giving the ranch to Jesse and Babs. He and Martha are going to find a temporary apartment in town until they can build on the forty acres out by the lake. He's deeding another fifty across the road to Cody and Ivy."

"Where did Martha live before? I never thought about that."

"With an elderly aunt and uncle. They didn't want her to get married because she did all the housework. Things are strained all around."

"This sounds like a good compromise. Is it?"

"Oh, it's great. Dad and Jesse aren't speaking. Jesse and I aren't speaking. Kirby doesn't think Louisa will marry him now. All I need to bat a thousand is for you to tell me to go pick out a wedding gift alone."

Hallie laughed. "Poor baby. Meet me at Bronson's at ten o'clock tomorrow. I know just the gift. Crystal plates to match a bowl I bought."

"That sounds easy. And you'll ride with me to the wedding?"

"Don't you want to know how much the crystal's going to cost you?"

"No. I trust you. Quit trying to find excuses."

"Why do you keep doing this, Chino? We can't seem to get along for more than five minutes. Maybe you should take Penny Beth." Even as the words left her lips, Hallie wanted to snatch them back. If he took the other woman, her own weekend would be ruined. Why was he being so quiet?

"Chino?" Hallie's query came too quickly. She hated his satisfied chuckle. "Oh, you. Awfully sure of yourself, aren't you?"

"Not at all. Name a time before you change your mind."

"You're the driver." But tell her he wasn't smug! She'd be darned if she'd give him more fuel to feed his already inflated ego.

"Is eight too early? We can stop halfway for lunch."

"I'll be ready. Oh, I never did congratulate you on third place."

"I still have to cook again before Terlingua. Guess I'm going to change my recipe. Kirby and Jess both say it lacks something."

"I thought you said you had a new secret ingredient."

"Didn't help. And no comments. There'll be no chili-talk this weekend, either."

"That's fair. It's late now, Chino. I'll see you tomorrow."

Next day, their shopping trip went fine until the clerk asked if they were signed up with the bridal registry. Straight-faced, Chino said no, but could they do it now? Of course he had no way of knowing the young clerk was in Hallie's English class. Or he said he didn't, anyway.

Hallie could just about hear the rumors starting again. She and Chino didn't part on the best of terms. Not after he felt it necessary to explain loudly that he was joking, and it turned out Penny Beth Frazier was in the next aisle.

By the end of the week, Hallie had managed to put the incident into perspective. Possibly since no one said a word about it at Glynnis's shower—which was hosted by Hallie and Evie and considered a big success by all concerned.

Friday morning, Chino arrived precisely on time. "Let me take your dress," he offered. "I'll hang it with my suit." He hefted her suitcase. "You sure this is the right bag? Never have met a woman yet who went *anywhere* with only one suitcase."

Hallie stopped where she was.

He held up a hand. "Before you say something snide, I'm thinking of my sisters-in-law, okay?"

"Believe it or not, I wasn't going to. I forgot my gift. If you put my bag in the car, I'll go get it." In fact, she'd deliberately left the gift in the house so she'd have a chance to slip the key under the mat without Chino's knowing. As it happened, Chino played right into her hands.

He was none the wiser when she joined him. He placed her gift beside his and opened the passenger door.

"I feel important," she said, "riding in this car again."

He smiled and eased behind the wheel. "You are important. Now, are we set? You bolted your doors and hid your chili recipe, right?"

"Roger!" She snapped off a salute.

"Say, you're in a good mood. No crank calls lately?"

"You said we weren't going to talk chili."

"We're not. I don't think the two are connected."

She lifted a brow. "And I do."

"Okay. What shall we discuss?"

"Are you men having a bachelor party tonight?"

"No. Did you hear the rehearsal dinner's going to be at the restaurant Joe will manage?"

"Chili?"

He chuckled. "Yep. 'Fraid so. Guess there's no avoiding it."

"I'll make do. Glynnis wouldn't give us a clue where they're going on the honeymoon. Do you know?"

"Local. Joe's starting work Monday."

"That's too bad. She got such lovely lingerie at her shower. One gown deserved at least a balcony in New Orleans' French Quarter."

"Ah."

"What's that mean?"

"You're a starry-eyed romantic."

She tilted her head to one side and smiled as she thought of Ram and Martha using her home as a honeymoon cottage. "Maybe I am."

"I'll bet the nightgown's white."

"Actually it was called iced champagne. Why?"

"My sisters-in-law both got these filmy white things." He studied her a moment. "You need jade silk like that blouse you had on the other night, only slinky, with little straps."

A wave of heat washed over Hallie. The vision was much too acute. She turned and looked out the side window. "Are you hungry?" she asked abruptly.

"Yeah," he muttered, passing a hand over his jaw. "But—" he grinned wickedly "—I could go for food, too. How about a burger?"

She refrained from answering, and he pulled into the next truck stop. After that they avoided talking about the wedding. As the miles fell away he asked why she'd decided to go into teaching and how she liked it. Soon they arrived at the modest hotel in Dallas where all the wedding guests would be staying.

"Let's check in," Chino suggested. "Then I'll bring my suit and your dress and give our bags to a bellman."

"Sounds good to me. I wonder if Evie and Daniel are here yet?"

"I doubt it. Dan said to meet in the lounge at six. Want to swim?" Before Hallie could decide, the desk clerk handed Chino a folded note. He passed the young man his credit card, read the note, then rubbed his jaw.

"What is it?" Hallie asked. "Not bad news?"

"It's from Jesse. He wants me to call right away. You don't suppose Dad had a—" Breaking off, Chino asked about a public phone.

Hallie had finished checking in by the time he returned. He still looked worried. "Is it Ram?" She touched his arm.

"Yes. According to Jesse, he and Martha have disappeared. Actually they missed lunch and Jess is feeling guilty. I told him not to worry unless they don't show for supper."

Hallie blanched. "Oh," she said in a small voice. She hadn't thought of this aspect, and she doubted if Ram had, either. What a dilemma. "Chino," she said, then stopped. It wasn't her place to break a confidence.

"Don't look so grim," he teased, running a finger down her nose. "It's not your problem. Dad's probably trying to teach Jesse a lesson."

Hallie went to her room, but she wasn't happy. She paced and tried calling her home twice. Of course they didn't answer. They wanted seclusion.

She dressed and went down to meet the others. No one seemed to notice that she was unusually quiet, especially since Daniel O'Malley was such a natural comedian.

Glynnis's parents and a couple of her siblings checked in just before it was time to go to the rehearsal and dinner. As the larger group assembled, Chino excused himself. "I promised to touch base with Jesse," he whispered to Hallie.

"Chino, wait." She made up her mind to explain. "Martha and Ram are hiding out at my place." She looked away. "They, uh, wanted some privacy. Can you calm Jesse without telling him where they are? I promised your dad."

"Of all the stupid, juvenile..." Then he threw back his head and laughed. "Like I said, you're a romantic. But Dad...well, I'll be damned."

Chino took care of everything and Hallie felt much better. She actually relaxed and enjoyed dinner. She chose Cody's winning chili cook-off recipe, which she had to admit was good. So was the service, and Hallie told Chino she was pleasantly surprised.

He grinned, kissing the tip of her nose just as Daniel suggested going to a club for a little dancing. The older members of the group declined. Everyone else went.

The club was upscale, the band above average. Chino was attentive. He was also an excellent dancer, and since Hallie wasn't, she didn't mind that he held her close. It helped her stay off his toes.

No, that wasn't really the reason. She liked it because people looked at them with that special smile that branded them a couple. She couldn't explain it, but anyone who'd been looked at like that would know. Chino nuzzled her ear. She let him twirl her until she felt light-headed. It was the kind of evening dreams were made of. The Cellar and chili cook-offs seemed far away and not very important.

They stayed until the club closed. The whole group returned to the motel feeling pretty mellow. Talk centered around the next morning's wedding.

"You know," Hallie said to Chino as they were left alone to ride the elevator to their floor, "I've never been to a morning wedding."

"It was Joe's idea, so his mother could come from the nursing home."

"He's thoughtful, isn't he. A nice man. Just right for Glynnis."

Chino stopped outside Hallie's room. He gathered her in his arms and kissed her gently. "Besides being a romantic, you have a sentimental streak in you a mile wide, Hallie Bergstrom,'' he whispered against her lips.

She smiled, leaned into him and closed her eyes. "Umm . . . is that bad?''

"No.'' He loosened his tie, placed a hand on the casing near her head and backed her against the door. "It's good. Invite me in—you'll see.''

Suddenly skittish, Hallie bolted. Too much history hung between them for her to risk rejection again. "G'night, Chino.'' She disappeared inside before he could persuade her. And she waited. If he tried again . . .

Chino stood for a moment staring at her closed door. Then he left.

Ultimately she went to bed feeling deflated.

THE BONNER WEDDING was as beautiful as any Hallie had ever seen. The sun streamed into the sanctuary through old stained-glass windows, forming a halo of rainbow hues around a radiant bride. Hallie was so caught up in the ceremony she almost forgot to hand Glynnis back her bouquet for the recessional—after the kiss. And what a kiss it was. Hallie's knees quivered. Or maybe that was because she looked up and saw Chino watching her, his dark eyes smoldering. It was all she could do to walk back down the aisle, holding tight to his arm.

Chino had his own problems. Each day he wanted her more, but the timing was never right. Like now, when they had a reception to attend. And by the time Glynnis changed into her going-away suit the mood had dissipated.

"Weddings are too short,'' Hallie whispered to Evie as they clung together, both wiping away tears.

"Well, be prepared,'' Evie murmured. "I'm going to have a high mass, the whole-nine-yards Catholic wedding. You'll be so tired of standing, kneeling and standing again, you'll think this wedding was bliss.''

"Are you trying to tell me something?'' Hallie asked sharply.

Evie's smile was dreamy. "I know this man is special, Hallie."

"It's weddings in general," Hallie told her. "They always make everyone sappy."

Chino overheard and wondered if she really meant what she said. After the newlyweds left, he and Daniel excused themselves to deal with "business," arranging to meet Hallie and Evie for dinner.

The two women spent the afternoon at a movie. When at last they met the men for dinner, Hallie decided Evie and Daniel might as well have skipped eating; they didn't seem to know anyone else was at the table. Right afterward, they took off alone.

"You're awfully quiet," Chino remarked on the way back to their hotel. "Post-wedding letdown?" he mused, massaging her tense neck.

"Ram and Martha had the right idea. Go to a justice of the peace. No fuss. No bother. That's what I'd do if I got married. Which I won't. See you in the morning, Chino. I'd like to leave by eight, okay?"

Once again he was left staring at her door. He considered breaking it down until it dawned on him—with Hallie, this was progress. Whistling, he moved off, tossed his room key in the air and, with a smile, caught it.

Back in his room, Chino took out a jeweler's box and gazed at matching diamond bands he'd just picked up. Hallie wasn't quite ready to accept a proposal, but he had a feeling it wouldn't be long. Complacent, he snapped the lid closed, stripped off his clothes and took an ice-cold shower.

Naked, in bed, he fantasized a bit about the other gift, now tucked in the bottom of his suitcase. Jade silk.

Chino's blood ran hot just imagining it against her skin. And his.

CHAPTER NINE

THE DRIVE BACK to Cedarville passed without incident. Hallie and Chino talked of inconsequential things until they entered the town limits. Then, unexpectedly, Chino broke his own rule. "We need to sit down with Penny Beth next week to discuss doing an article about us calling off our chili dispute."

Hallie turned swiftly. "Are we?"

He waved a hand. "It's a moot point now, don't you think? I'm restoring the Cellar to ensure its historical value like you wanted."

"Yes, but what about our literary club? We liked the coffeehouse."

"The original tavern had a meeting room. We'll restore it. But let's get back to the chili thing. In case you haven't heard, there's a duel shaping up between Hank Edwards and me. Our rivalry goes back to football days. Since the Chilympiad he's been bragging about beating me." Chino flashed her a determined look. "I see no earthly reason for you to suffer the humility of defeat in all this."

"Who says I'll be defeated?" Hallie's head came up.

"Come on. You're using a domestic recipe. The judges at Terlingua aren't looking for a nice family dish. They go for stick-to-the-ribs stuff. Folks who cook *Behind the Store* are serious Texas chili-heads. We aren't in it for charity like the CASI crowd, although I do admire their dedication. We don't take prize money for ourselves like the ICS finalists in California, either. Their winner takes home twenty-five thousand or more." He shook his head. "Not us. With our group it's the integrity of no-bean chili. And sometimes the competition gets pretty heated and personal."

"I see," she said icily as he pulled into her driveway. "What we're talking about here is your good-ol'-boy network in all its glory—especially with those nebulous Tolbert's rules. Right?"

Chino noticed the way her blue eyes had erupted into indignant flames. "I didn't mean to imply that we exclude women. I was merely trying to give *you* an easy out." He stopped the car near her back door.

Hallie unbuckled her seat belt, reached into the back seat and snatched up her dress and suitcase. She almost smacked him on the head as she hauled both items to the front.

"Hey. I'll get those." He struggled to unsnap his own seat belt, which was now buried under her dress.

"Don't bother," she said, flouncing out and pulling her things after her. "And don't write off my chili yet, buster. If you so much as hint to Penny Beth Frazier that I don't intend to try for first place in Terlingua, I'll sue you for libel."

"Damn it, Hallie. I didn't mean—" Chino's words were cut off by the loud slam of her door. By the time he'd untangled his long legs from the low-slung sports car, her house door banged equally hard. He stood for a moment, drumming his fingers on the car's metal roof.

She stuck her head outside again and yelled, "You are so unbelievably transparent, Chino. Do you think people are too dense to see what's behind this sudden switch? You simply can't stand that Serita's taken up with Hank Edwards. Penny Beth said you weren't jealous. Ha! Was *she* off base." With that, Hallie withdrew, slamming her back door.

"You're the one who's off base," he shouted, starting toward her house. Then, thinking better of it, he stopped. If she couldn't— If she thought for a minute that this was about Serita, then, damn it, Hallie Bergstrom wasn't the woman he thought.

Furious, Chino climbed back into his car. He gunned the engine and tore out of her driveway, slowing only when he hit the main road. "Tolbert's rules are not nebulous," he muttered.

Nose glued to her kitchen window, Hallie watched him leave. It was a while before she realized her cheeks were damp. Angrily she scrubbed at the unwanted tears. He'd recognized the truth soon enough, but apparently he hadn't expected *her* to be so astute. Let him play macho games with Hank; she'd beat them both in Terlingua. Gram's chili was good. Darn good.

The best way to ensure winning, Hallie decided as she put away her things, was to walk away from Luckenbach with first place. Thoroughly incensed, she almost missed seeing the envelope taped to Gram's bedroom door. A thank-you card from Ram and Martha, as it turned out. One of them had drawn two happy faces at the bottom. That dragged a laugh out of her.

She nudged the bedroom door open, not quite sure what to expect—a tumbled bed at the very least, she supposed. The room didn't have a single thing out of place. A second scribbled message lying on the dresser indicated that Martha had laundered the sheets and remade the bed.

Somehow Hallie didn't think she'd be inclined to launder sheets on *her* honeymoon. But then, what did she know about honeymoons? Or, for that matter, about relationships, as Chino had pointed out the other day. She left Gram's room, quietly closing the door. It would be nice to have someone care—the way Jesse Delgado had stood up for Babs, and Ram for Martha out at the ranch that evening. Cody's first thought had been to protect his wife, Ivy, and Jesse's children from unpleasantness.

Hallie folded the note and tucked it into her jeans pocket. Her mistake was in comparing herself with the Delgado women. Why did she? Chino hadn't given her any reason to hope. Not even Friday night after the dance, when he'd invited himself into her hotel room. That night there'd been magic in the air. Enough so she actually held her breath waiting—wanting him to knock and ask again. A dry laugh caught in her throat. Just as well he hadn't. Otherwise these tears she couldn't seem to halt would be tears of regret.

In the week that followed, Hallie felt as forlorn as she ever had. With Glynnis in Dallas and Evie burning up the roads between Cedarville and San Antonio in her growing relationship with Daniel O'Malley, Hallie was forced to fall back on her own resources. She even worked on new lesson plans.

By Thursday some semblance of contentment had returned. As a diversion, she spent the afternoon experimenting with variations to Gram's chili. She concluded that the original recipe tasted best. Carefully she measured the ingredients to take to Luckenbach the next day.

In a way it wasn't surprising that her anonymous caller got into action again that night and robbed her of much-needed sleep. Come dawn, her eyes were gritty and red-rimmed. More determined than ever, she packed her tent-trailer and hit the road just as the sun streaked the eastern sky in glorious shades of lavender and pink. Too glorious, considering her feelings. Her heart just wasn't in this trip, since it was patently obvious that her caller had to be Chino. Who else knew she was going to the women's event? Or more to the point, who else cared?

As Hallie traversed the lonely ribbon of highway winding through the rolling foothills, she thought about all the years she'd wasted pining for Chino. Even now, when it was clear what a rat he was, she wondered if it was possible to banish him completely from her mind, from her nightly dreams, from her heart where for ten years he'd been firmly entrenched.

Immersed in her thoughts, Hallie drove past the sign to Luckenbach. Forced to backtrack, she relegated Chino to a dark recess in her heart and concentrated, instead, on finding the cook site. It wasn't hard. There was a long line of RVs to follow.

Nice, Hallie thought as she craned her neck to give the park a once-over. Banners welcoming cook-off entrants waved merrily in the breeze. Overhead, barn swallows swooped in precision aerobatics. She smiled, a smile that widened once she discovered Mama Claire—with a free space right beside her, too. Their paths hadn't crossed in a while.

"Hey, Classy Lassie," the older woman greeted her. "How the heck you been?"

"Fine," Hallie answered. "Have you switched from brisket to chili?"

"I have, at that. Dutch has this hare-brained scheme to travel around California and the Northwest next year following cook-offs. He says if I cook, too, we'll double our chances of winning the world championship. And it's a way to see some new country. I've been on the chili circuit every weekend lately. Almost have enough points to do Terlingua."

"Me, too." Hallie said as she unrolled her awning. "Personally, I'm glad you're here." She recounted some of the things that had happened.

Mama Claire commiserated, but stood up for Chino all the same. "Lassie, I know Chili Man. You're barkin' up the wrong tree."

Hallie just shrugged.

Throughout the afternoon, the women chatted about other things. Later, as they sipped spiced cider outside Mama Claire's camper, Hallie said, "Seems to be more frivolity here. Less emphasis on points. Why is that?"

"A chance for the ladies to kick up their heels without the old ball and chain. The way our menfolk did for so many years before they opened chili cook-offs to women. There'll be entertainment tonight. And cowboys. We're gonna choose a hunk to compete in the Mr. Terlingua contest." She rolled her eyes. "Before this they've only had *Miss* Terlingua. You know, the wet T-shirt type. Last year the ladies demanded equal treatment. Wanna check out muscled chests and sexy buns?" Mama winked, then snapped her fingers. "Say, you oughtta talk Chili Man into entering. I've never seen him without a shirt, mind you, but the way that man walks is pure sinful.''

Hallie smiled. ''I don't disagree, but he'd never do it. In some ways, he's kind of old-fashioned.''

''A gentleman, you mean? Don't complain. Too few left, if you ask me.''

''We aren't an item, Mama Claire. He's interested in someone else.'' Hallie had to force that past a big lump in her throat.

''Too bad, but if you mean that dark-haired hussy a coupla rows over, well, I wouldn't fret. I heard them having words earlier.''

''Chino's here?'' Hallie couldn't hide her shock.

''Yep. Saw him myself. But he didn't see me, 'cause I didn't like the mouth on that snippy miss. Not his type at all. Hard as granite, that one.''

''If it's not too obvious, would you point her out?'' Mama Claire did, and Hallie's stomach dropped. ''That's his ex-wife,'' Hallie whispered. ''I didn't know she competed.''

The older woman wrinkled her nose. ''Smart man, dumping her. They ain't gettin' back together, I tell ya. So quit worryin', gal.''

Hallie didn't say the worrisome part was finding them *both* here. But the moment to confide passed and talk turned to other things.

Dusk fell. Hallie still hadn't laid eyes on Chino. She ran into Serita once in the bathroom, though. Chino's ex looked right through her. Hallie wished the tight knot in her stomach would ease. As a precautionary measure, she locked all her ingredients in her truck for the night, along with her stove.

Mama Claire tried again to talk Hallie into joining her for the evening's entertainment. ''Do you good to ogle cowboys, lass.''

Hallie declined. Ogling men had never been her style, and things being what they were, she felt she'd be better served standing guard over her outfit. That was her intention. But after sleeping poorly the night before, ten o'clock found her dead to the world.

She wouldn't have slept a wink had she known that Chino returned with Mama Claire and the two of them sat drinking coffee for hours. Even when the older woman turned in, Chino stayed, slouched in a very uncomfortable lawn chair, his only company a large thermos of black coffee. He didn't leave until Mama Claire came out in the morning to start her chili.

Hallie slept until her alarm sounded. Yawning, she stuck her head out of the trailer and squinted at her bustling neighbor. "I can't believe it's morning." She covered another yawn. "Normally I don't get a whole night's sleep."

"No wonder, what with all those phone calls you been gettin'." Claire waved a beringed hand. "You didn't tell me about those creeps trashin' your gear up in Fort Worth. It wasn't Chili Man. Why, he's worried half-sick, lassie. Made me promise to keep my eyes open today."

"Chino Delgado has ulterior motives for everything he does. There's a lot you don't know, Mama. I'm afraid I can't trust him." Hallie's tone was filled with sadness.

But the older woman didn't listen. "Don't you think overhearing those bozos was a mite coincidental?" Mama Claire asked.

This time Hallie was the one not listening. She went back inside, dressed, then set about braising her meat. Around noon, she began having problems with her stove. If she turned the gas as low as she needed, the burner went out. When set high enough to keep a flame, it was too hot.

Mama Claire responded to Hallie's mutterings by coming over to take a look. "Acts like the line is crimped," she said after some deliberation.

Hallie threw up her hands and turned off the burner. "Well, that's that. If I hadn't locked everything in my truck last night, I'd swear Chino was responsible. It's typical of what happens when he's around."

"Rat poop!" Mama Claire snapped. "Like as not you banged the stove stuffin' it into the cab last night. Bring your pot over here. I got a four-burner unit. Plenty of room."

"That's awfully nice of you. Are you sure?"

"Dutch and me, we've seen a lot during the years we been cookin'. But even in the old days—the chili wars—nobody did anybody dirt. Oh, folks blew a lot of hot air, but the truth is, even the first big cook-off ended in a tie. The box with the final scores just kinda disappeared, if you know what I mean. Nobody wanted to hurt the feelins of that ol' boy from back East who claimed his chili was the best. Not even if he did use beans."

Hallie carried her pot over and placed it on a back burner. As she thanked Mama Claire again for her generosity, they heard laughter, coupled with a commotion near the park entrance. Both women stepped beneath Hallie's awning and shaded their eyes, trying to see what was going on.

Just then three masked horsemen galloped past.

"Probably trick riders," Mama Claire said. "Maybe rope tricks." She pointed as the three began swinging lariats.

Hallie braced a hand on a pole. Ropers fascinated her. All three riders were headed back now, coiled ropes whistling in ever-widening circles above their heads. They were almost abreast of her, and she was staring directly into the sun, when one of them seemed to lose control of his horse. She jumped back, but the rump of the bay gelding slammed against an awning brace. The slender pole crumpled, throwing Hallie to the ground. She struck the edge of her unstable metal table and everything went flying. Loose canvas unfurled and covered her like a shroud.

Mama Claire barely managed to escape.

Struggling to find a way out, Hallie heard shouts and running feet. Someone with strong arms dragged her from under the debris and cradled her close to a pounding heart. Hallie found it difficult to clear her head—partly because her savior wore the masculine scent she loved. Brushing hair from her eyes, she looked up into sable eyes. But of course, she thought bitterly. She might have known Chino would be around to view his handiwork.

"Tell me you aren't hurt," he demanded, running unsteady hands down her arms and legs. Straightening, he drew a knuckle lightly over a bruise on her cheek. "Don't look at me like that," he pleaded.

"Who were those masked men?" a bystander joked.

"Too rude to leave silver bullets," another added. "The jerks didn't even stop to see if the little lady was hurt."

Mama Claire trotted up to Chino. "I'm plumb sorry, Chili Man. It all happened so fast. It musta been those fellas your brother heard talkin'."

"What fellows?" Hallie wrested herself out of Chino's hold. "Oh, no, look what you've done now!" she cried, her gaze falling on the mess.

"Not me, Hallie." Chino's fingers bit into her arm as he hauled her around to face him. "Clear out, everyone," he ordered in a deadly tone. "If you want to help, find someone who knows those riders."

The onlookers scattered. Hallie suddenly swayed like a willow sapling in a high wind. "You got an extra chair?" Chino asked Mama Claire. She handed him the one he'd sat in all night, and he gently pushed Hallie into it. His jaw tensed. "Listen to me, Hallie. I swear I didn't have anything to do with this."

She lifted a pale face and delivered a censorious look.

"Hear me out." He knelt beside her. "Thursday, Cody was at the Cellar playing darts. Three characters dropped in, had a few brews and started jawing about the women's cook-off. Cody was set to leave until he heard my name. He caught enough to know they were planning something for Luckenbach that involved you and me. Cody pumped them a bit, but they clammed up and took off. I came to keep an eye out, for all the good it did."

Hallie sagged, but her arms crept around his neck. "One of them did look familiar, Chino. I think the bearded guy was in Fort Worth."

"Damn it, they've ruined your chili again, too. I'm so sorry, honey. Who'd guess they'd strike in broad daylight?"

"My chili is fine," she said, sitting upright. "Sorry to disappoint you."

"Disappoint me?" His lips thinned. "I see. You don't believe a word I've said."

"I don't know what to believe." Her voice broke. She stood, and on legs not yet steady went to stir her chili.

Chino followed. He wrapped her in his arms again. "Don't cry. Oh, God, don't cry. I promise we'll find them if it's the last thing I do."

"I'm too mad to cry," Hallie declared.

"If I was you, Chili Man," Mama Claire suggested, "I'd start with your ex. Saw her during the to-do. She looked right smug."

"Serita?" Chino sounded appalled. "But why?"

"Dutch says some folks are just naturally mean-spirited. Maybe she's a sore loser."

Chino reached up and idly rubbed the back of Hallie's neck. "There's no love lost between Serita and me, but our parting was mutual. That's the God's truth, Hallie." He stared into her eyes a moment, then pulled her against him. "In all honesty, I don't think she's smart enough to mastermind something this complex."

Hallie clung to him, drawing strength from his steady heartbeat. "Who, then, and why me?" she whispered.

"I don't know." His hold tightened, becoming almost fierce. He kissed the top of her head and combed his fingers through her hair. "But, Hallie, when they hurt you . . . they hurt me."

"Maybe it was accidental," she said, burrowing into his chest like a rabbit.

Mama Claire cleared her throat. "Hate to break this up, kids, but Hallie's chili is gettin' thick. I know you probably don't want an old woman's opinion, lassie, but it appears somebody's tryin' real hard to make you lose. If it was me, I'd do my best to prove 'em wrong."

Chino reluctantly loosened his grip. "In the beginning I discounted the calls. Old-timers can be pretty mule-headed when it comes to newcomers and chili, but usually all in fun.

Now, I just don't know. Think I'll nose around while you cook. Promise me neither of you ladies will leave the other alone until I get back.''

Both women agreed.

Chino dropped a light kiss on the tip of Hallie's nose.

She desperately wanted to believe he was sincere and managed a weak smile.

He was gone most of the afternoon, arriving back shortly after she'd dumped her secret ingredient into the bubbling pot.

"Boy, that smells good." He grabbed a fork and helped himself to a bite. "Damn. I still can't identify the taste. Sweet, yet it has a bite. Will you ever tell me?"

"Maybe," Hallie said.

"Just how bad do you want to know, boy?" Mama Claire asked him, hooting with laughter.

Hallie didn't think the comment was funny. It gave her the shivers.

Mama Claire asked if she could try a spoonful. "Tastes like a winner, gal," she said, smacking her lips. "Darned if I know what makes that flavor. Sort of like cranberry, but not quite."

Afraid she'd slip if they both started badgering her, Hallie changed the subject. "Did you find out anything about those riders, Chino?"

"Only that they apparently came together. One truck, one trailer. And they didn't unsaddle when they left. It wasn't accidental, Hallie."

Hallie blanched, but tried to put up a good front.

Chino noticed. Immediately he started making wild and outrageous guesses as to what her secret substance might be. Soon he had both women in stitches.

Almost before they knew it, it was time for the judging.

Chino checked Hallie's marked cup. "For any sign of tampering," he said when she questioned him. Satisfied nothing was amiss, he offered to stay behind while the women took their full cups to the judges.

In spite of everything, Hallie had a good feeling about her chili. The consistency was thick, the aroma rich. She thought it smelled the way Gram's always had, and she suffered a moment's nostalgia.

She crossed her fingers. If it was good enough to take first place, she wouldn't have to run afoul of those men again. At least not until Terlingua. And Ram and Martha would be there. She'd feel a whole lot safer with them around, even if they were Delgados.

But she didn't win first place. A sweet, grandmotherly woman from San Angelo walked away with that honor. Hallie's entry came in second, which meant she was two points away from qualifying. And still one point behind Chino.

Mama Claire was both surprised and happy when her chili took fourth. "Didn't expect it," she told Chino back in camp. "So where you two gonna go next? Maybe we can sort of team up. You know, camp together again."

Chino waltzed Hallie around in circles, exclaiming over her placing. He sobered at Mama Claire's question, but kept Hallie tucked beneath one arm as he considered. "Rattlesnake Gulch might be good," he finally said. "Flat, desolate country. It would be hard for our three friends to get in or out as easily as they did here. Why don't you look over the list, Hallie? Then you choose."

"Rattlesnake— I don't know, Chino. Name some other places."

He laughed. "Some other options are Abilene or Austin, if you want to cook on ye olde Capitol's lawn. But they've already held the rattlesnake roundup, so I think the Gulch would be best."

"Whoa! Rattlesnake roundup? Are you kidding me?"

Mama Claire chuckled. "He's tellin' it true, lassie. Where've you been all your life? They give prizes for the biggest snake, the longest, the most rattles—that sort of thing. Dutch loves it."

"He would," Chino said.

"I teach literature, not zoology," Hallie reminded him.

Still laughing, Chino filled her in. "Originally, some of the big ranchers paid cowboys to rid the open range of rattlers. Since cowboys would rather play games and compete against each other than work for wages, it sort of evolved into a yearly contest. Anyway, what snakes are left will be more afraid of us than we are of them. What do you say, shall we try the Gulch?"

Hallie remained apprehensive until Mama Claire pointed out how crowded Austin was and said that even in Abilene it might be hard to stay together. In the end, Hallie went along with Rattlesnake Gulch.

"Good. Now that's settled, let's get you packed. I'm going to follow you home. No, forget it," Chino said flatly as Hallie started to object. "Won't do you any good. Hassle me too much, woman, and I'll simply move in with you until the Terlingua competition is over."

Hallie blushed. To cover her discomfort, she accused him of getting bossy like his dad.

Chino grinned. "Don't want a roommate, huh? Guess you aren't as liberal as your friend, Evie."

"What?"

"Evie. She's moving in with Daniel this weekend. Didn't you know?"

Hallie looked at him as if he were two bricks short of a full load.

"You didn't," he said. "Sorry, I just assumed . . . Well, hell, they're both adults. Why are you looking so horrified?"

"I . . . it simply comes as a surprise. That makes two friends—two colleagues—leaving before school starts." She spun away, a void in the pit of her stomach. What really hurt was that Evie hadn't said a word. "Think I'll just clean up," Hallie murmured. "Don't wait for me, Chino."

"No. You won't get rid of me so easily this time, Hallie."

And indeed, once he'd seen her safely home, Chino stuck around to help her unload. "I'll straighten these poles and fix whatever other damage those jokers did," he said, lips set and eyes flashing as they lit on the bruise on her cheek. "I won't say no if you invite me to dinner, either."

Hallie shifted, shy once again in the face of his overwhelming masculine intensity. "Some people will do anything for chocolate chip cookies," she grumbled, trying to lighten the mood.

He traced a finger along her jaw. "Would you run if I told you chocolate chip cookies—even ones as delectable as yours—have nothing to do with it?"

His admission and the look on his face dissolved the last of Hallie's suspicions that he'd been involved in what had happened. It also changed the rules of the game. She didn't know if she was ready, not when she'd just spent weeks trying to get him out of her system.

Moved beyond words by the warmth of his caring, she lowered her gaze and put an icy palm over his hand—the hand that still cupped her cheek.

Chino sensed her indecision. He stepped closer, and his thumbs outlined her cheekbones. "It's okay," he murmured. "We'll take it as slow or as fast as you like. We're not on any timetable." He kissed her then, a prolonged, delicious melding of lips and bodies.

Hallie took everything he offered and wanted more as he pulled back with an almost apologetic quirk at one corner of his mouth.

Unfamiliar emotions raced through her veins. She felt bereft...dissatisfied. For his part, Chino had returned so easily to the chore he'd left, Hallie stood there uncertainly, not knowing what to think. But because he'd already bent to the task of repairing her trailer, she turned after a moment and hurried back into the house.

Inside, she leaned against the door and pressed shaking hands tight to her stomach.

For the first time in her life, Hallie couldn't think of a single appropriate Gram-ism. Of course, Gram had been big on believing food cured whatever ailed a person. That was a solution of sorts. Chino said he was hungry, so even though Hallie had a knot the size of Maine in her stomach, she set about fixing him the most filling meal anyone could whip up on such short notice.

CHAPTER TEN

A FEW MOMENTS before her meat loaf was browned to perfection, Hallie called Chino inside to wash up. There was something so intimate about doing that, her stomach went all queasy again.

"Yum," he exclaimed the moment he stepped through the door. "Does that ever smell good. What's cooking?"

"Meat loaf. To hear you talk, Chino, all food smells wonderful. Either you like the smell better than the taste or you work off a lot of calories." She ran an appreciative eye over his firm chest and flat stomach, then felt her cheeks redden as he caught her and smiled.

Both laughed self-consciously.

As he headed down the hall to the bathroom, Hallie hurried back to peek in the oven.

The telephone rang just as he returned to the kitchen, running a hand through his damp hair.

They exchanged worried glances, she with pot holders poised over a hot dish in the oven, he hesitating in the doorway. "Let the machine pick it up," he suggested, buttoning a cuff of his shirt.

"Can't. I never got around to buying a new tape."

"Damn." In two strides, he crossed the room and yanked up the receiver. "Hello," he growled, intending to sound gruff.

Hallie watched a strange expression cross his face.

"Oh, Evie, sorry. Chino here. No, I'm not fighting with Hallie. I thought you were her crank caller. Could she call you back? We're about to eat. No?" He covered the mouthpiece. "She says it's important."

"Hi, Evie." Hallie's greeting was cool. She couldn't deny that her friend's secrecy had hurt. "Chino told me your news."

Chino stepped behind her and began a slow massage of her tense shoulders as she listened intently. Every so often she interjected something like, "No kidding," until at last she said, "I'll give it some thought, Evie. Goodbye. And Evie...good luck."

"Are you all right?" he asked when Hallie stared out the window, her eyes misty.

"I never knew she applied for a teaching job in San Antonio last year. Apparently one just opened up and they hired her. She's not moving in with Daniel. He has a garage apartment that he's leasing her for a good price." Hallie blinked and wiped away a tear.

"That's bad?" Confused, Chino gathered both her hands in his, lifted them to his lips and kissed her knuckles. "I guess I jumped to conclusions. I admit my mind was on other things when Daniel phoned, but I'm afraid I don't understand why you're crying." He released one of her hands and brushed at a tear caught in the curve of her cheek.

"It's silly but, well, the three of us were a team. Our colleagues never bucked the system, but we did—for the kids. I'm happy for Evie if this is what she wants, but I keep thinking about our kids. And our classrooms, which we just got the administration to paint. I'm the only one who'll be here to enjoy them."

Chino pieced together what she was saying. It hurt him to see her this way. He pulled her into his arms and kissed her eyelids closed. "I think I understand. You feel abandoned. Let down. My brothers and I went through something like that when our mom died. I'll listen if you like." He leaned back, looking grave. "It's talk or rebel, Hallie. Believe me, I know, and I'm not sure Cedarville High can handle another rebellion." He winked.

She considered what might have prompted such a comment, punched him lightly on one arm and escaped to the stove. "Rebel, is it? Let's eat. If I'm going to raise hell *and* put the make on half the men in town, I'll definitely need more energy. That *is* the route Jesse, Cody and you took, isn't it?"

He coughed.

Smiling, she lifted a sheet of overbrowned biscuits from the oven and set them on the table between a steaming meat loaf and a fresh green salad.

"I didn't sleep around," he muttered. "Not after I met you."

"Right," she drawled. "You got married, instead."

Chino snagged her arm before she sat. "You're the only woman who's ever mattered since the day you ran full tilt out of the school office and smacked right into me—10 a.m., September fourteenth." In voice husky with feeling, he added the year.

Stunned, Hallie dropped into her chair.

He let her arm slide through his fingers and took a seat across the table, calmly unfurling his napkin. "Are you surprised I remembered the date?"

She was more than surprised. She was shocked. Carefully avoiding his gaze, she offered him a warm biscuit.

"I was in love with you, Hallie," he said, forcing her gaze up. "You were the first good thing to come into my life in a long time. The first innocent, too," he said wryly. "Add that to the fact you resembled my mother, well, it plain scared the hell out of me. I wish I could turn back the clock. Do things differently." His voice lowered. "But I can't."

Her fingers trembled. She dropped the biscuit and crushed her napkin. "I didn't know," she whispered, looking at her plate. "At first I felt rejected. Then when you married Serita, I felt betrayed."

"I'm sorry, Hallie." Reaching across the table, he stilled her nervous fingers. "Is that why you never dated in college?"

"How do you know I never dated? Don't tell me you kept tabs."

He shook his head. "I wish I had. But it was a bad time for me. Work. School. Serita. My own guilt was a trial. No, Glynnis told me. But don't blame her. She accused me of ruining your life."

"Glynnis exaggerates. My life wasn't exactly *ruined.*" Hallie fought to hang on to a thread of self-respect. "Anyway, as you said, talking won't change history. Eat—the food's getting cold."

Chino withdrew his hand and began to fill his plate. "I made a lot of mistakes, Hallie. Is there a chance to start over?"

"Start what?" She paused, the platter of meat loaf wavering over the table.

He guided a slice to his plate. "Us," he murmured. "Dating. A real courtship."

Hallie's jaw sagged. "But... but, what about Serita and Penny Beth?"

Chino arched a brow. "What about them?"

"Serita's still following you. Don't deny it. Mama Claire saw you two talking Saturday. And Babs is pushing for you to marry Penny Beth."

"Serita is not following me. She's taken up with Hank Edwards. I felt honor bound to tell her a few things about Hank, but she didn't want to listen. And Penny Beth Frazier has never been anything but an acquaintance."

Hallie watched him taste the meat loaf. "What if we end up cooking against one another in the final round, Chino? I'm not quitting."

He held up both palms. "Not an issue."

She passed him the salad, then picked up her fork and began to eat.

"So?" he demanded. "What's the verdict?"

Hallie chewed and swallowed. Her flesh still tingled from the memory of his touch. "Yes. I'd like to start over. I'd like it a lot," she said softly.

"All right!" He released a breath he'd been unconsciously holding. Rising, Chino circled the table, tilted her chin and kissed her thoroughly.

"I probably taste like salad," she protested.

"Nothing ever tasted better," he said, lifting her up and into his arms.

Her napkin slid from her lap to the floor. Dinner grew cold. Chino was nibbling his way down her neck and lower to the pulse throbbing wildly in her throat when the telephone shrilled, shattering the moment.

Reluctantly he let her go to answer it.

Hallie's dreamy hello was met with silence. She said hello again, her voice rising.

Chino crossed the room and pulled the receiver from her grasp. "Who is this?" he shouted, anger coloring his words. "Hear this. If anything happens to this woman or her chili between now and Terlingua, I promise you you'll be dealing with *all* the Delgados." He heard smothered laughter, then a distinct click as the caller disconnected. Left with a vacant hum, he slammed the phone down in frustration. "They're gone," he said, massaging tension from the back of his neck. "They heard me," he said grimly. "I hope they do show. I'd love to get my hands on the bastards."

"I don't want to go to Rattlesnake Gulch, Chino."

He ran his fingers up her bare arms, chasing away the gooseflesh that had suddenly appeared. "Okay. I think you're right. We should skip the cook-offs for a while. Forget the rest of August. Pick one in September. If, by chance, neither of us places, there'll still be a few in October. What do you say?"

"School starts in September. I'll be busy."

"It'd be weekends. There's one mid-September in Lost Maples Park. We wouldn't have far to drive, and the trees may be changing colors by then."

"Oh, yes." Her eyes sparked with interest. "Glynnis took her art class there to sketch the bigtooth maples. It's so close, yet I've never found time to visit. I'd like that, Chino."

"Then it's settled. I'll call Mama Claire and cancel. But let's not tell anyone our plans. If someone starts asking questions, we may have our suspect. Meanwhile, you get a new tape and screen all your calls.''

Hallie shivered. "This is Cedarville—you sound so cloak-and-dagger.''

"Would you consider coming to San Antonio for a couple of weeks?'' he said brightly to mask his concern. "Help me plan the Labor Day party I always throw for home-office employees.''

"Me? Deal with caterers who saw you undressing me in the middle of your kitchen? I think not.''

Chino laughed. "There are other catering companies.''

She eyed him narrowly. "I might be more inclined to come if you simply promised not to undress me in the kitchen.''

"You've got it.'' He flashed a two-fingered salute. "I promise to confine undressing to the bedroom.''

Hallie arched a brow and tapped her toe. "Chino.''

"Oh, you want a hands-off promise? Okay, I'll be exemplary. You can have a whole wing to yourself. How's that for honor?''

She smiled. "Who could refuse an offer like that? And I do need to shop for school clothes. No monkey business, though, Chino. I mean it.''

"Word of honor. Now I'll do these dishes while you go pack a bag.''

BY THE END of her first week in San Antonio, Hallie could only say he was as good as his word—thoughtful, considerate, charming. After that, she relaxed and relished her role as temporary lady of the manor.

One evening toward the latter part of the second week, after she'd spent the day helping Evie move into her new place, Chino came in late from the office and found her asleep in front of the television. He stripped off his jacket and tie, then totally lost his resolve and kissed her into wakefulness.

Awakened suddenly from a pleasant dream that involved him, Hallie wound her arms around his neck and returned his ardent kisses.

Several times his fingers strayed to the zipper of her dress. Each time he groaned and drew back, at last tearing himself away to go stand beside the fireplace. "I'm afraid I have monkey business in mind, Hallie. How about fixing coffee before I break my word?"

Because her own principles were badly shaken, Hallie said nothing. She simply did as he asked.

From then on, Chino made certain they were busy in the evenings. In fact, he planned so many activities and outings that Labor Day weekend sneaked up on Hallie.

She got up one Saturday morning and discovered this was the night of Chino's staff party. Tomorrow she'd be going back to Cedarville. Alone. But that didn't mean she couldn't enjoy their last evening together.

Joe and Glynnis flew in, and although Daniel wasn't technically an employee, he and Evie had also been invited. Chino spent the evening with a casual arm draped around Hallie's waist. Being at his side felt so right, so comfortable. Yet Hallie wasn't at all sure where their relationship stood now. Had anything really changed?

She was still struggling with her thoughts when he ushered his last guest out. And the mood continued as he loosened his tie and she picked up wineglasses.

"Leave those," he instructed, stepping over to run both hands up her half-bare back. "Did I mention how beautiful you are tonight?"

She shifted to let him nuzzle her ear. The glasses clinked musically.

"I didn't think I'd like your hair up," he said, cocking his head to stare intently at her. "But it's classy. Dutch named you right," he murmured, bending to lay a moist trail of kisses along the edges of her strapless black dress. "Classy Lassie."

The glasses rattled as Hallie's knees turned to pudding. "That reminds me," she said, her voice too high, "Ivy called this afternoon. She said our confirmations to cook at Lost Maples came to the ranch yesterday.''

He straightened, a frown marring his brow. "I listed this address for both of us. Why do you suppose they were mailed to the ranch?"

She set the glasses aside. "Surely you don't suspect anyone in your family?"

He ran a hand over shadowy stubble, courtesy of the late hour. "Of course not, but I wasn't taking chances this time. Maybe I'll follow you back and pick them up." He wrapped her in his arms again and sighed. "I'm sure there's nothing wrong. It's just ... I'm going to Oklahoma City for a couple of weeks and you'll be in Cedarville alone."

"Oklahoma City? Whatever for?"

"Someone's interested in picking up a franchise. Kirby was going to go, but it's Louisa's birthday." A smile twitched at the corners of Chino's lips. "I'll enjoy having him in my debt."

Hallie laughed around a yawn.

"Come with me," he said urgently, catching her earlobe between his teeth, his breath warming her neck.

"To Oklahoma? Oh, Chino, I can't. School's starting, and I have to move a ton of books back into those newly painted rooms I mentioned. Otherwise..."

He pounced on what she'd left unsaid. "I heard Evie tell you one of the high schools here is looking for an English teacher. What do you think?"

Hallie slipped from his arms. Feeling out of her depth again, she edged toward the stairs. "I, uh, think it's time for bed."

He shoved his hands into his pockets. "Yours or mine?"

"They're both yours, Chino." Hallie hesitated, a hand on the banister. "You know, Gram always said courtships should build a solid foundation."

"Solid foundations are built on trust, Hallie. The fact that we're even having this discussion tells me you still don't trust me. Go to bed," he said wearily. "I'll see you in the morning." Turning away, he picked up a crystal decanter and splashed three fingers of amber liquid into a squat glass.

Hallie gripped the railing. *But she did trust him. Didn't she?* Then, because he didn't turn around, she made her way slowly up the stairs. *She loved him.* Gram had also said love and trust went hand in hand. Once, Hallie would have trusted him with her life—with her body. So why this hesitation? Confused and unhappy, she went to bed.

An hour or so later, Chino paused outside her door. He turned the knob, intending to look in on her—and only to look. It was locked. He was disappointed that she felt the need to barricade herself from him. He stalked off to his room. What if they never found out who was behind the chili mischief? It didn't bode well for their relationship. Toward morning, he fell into a troubled sleep.

Hallie awoke refreshed and eager to tell Chino that all her doubts had vanished overnight. She felt sure now that he'd had no part in any of the nonsense taking place. She had no idea who was responsible, only a firm conviction that it wasn't Chino.

Downstairs, the caterers were cleaning up. Chino didn't come down, though, until just before it was time to leave. He was carrying his bag for the Oklahoma trip and seemed too preoccupied for Hallie to talk to him.

She assumed when he'd said he would follow her home that he'd meant that literally. When he merely honked at the Cedarville crossroads and turned toward the ranch, she was put out. Unless he planned to drop by afterward...

But apparently not. The afternoon waned and Hallie's spirits plummeted.

Days passed without her hearing from him. She threw her energy into school. Never had she missed her friends so acutely as when she carried that first load of books down a hall smelling of new paint.

However, the moment she entered her homeroom, flipped on the light and discovered the green walls had been replaced with soft ivory only as high as a man could reach without a ladder, she had to laugh. It was so typical. When she checked the other rooms and found them the same, it seemed her life again had a purpose.

She stormed down to the office and dragged back a protesting principal. He stammered apologies. She wanted solutions. In the end she told him, "You supply the paint and I'll do the work myself."

He objected, but caved in the moment she threatened another trip to the board. Thing was, there was no one with whom she could share her triumph. Returning home for a second load of books, she took time out to call Glynnis and Evie. Neither answered. As a last resort she called Chino's father, only to have Babs tell her he and Martha had moved into an apartment—and their phone number was unlisted. Babs wasn't about to give it to her. Yet if Jesse's wife hadn't rung off, Hallie would have broken down and asked about Chino.

The next afternoon she launched a whirlwind attack on the classrooms.

September seemed to melt away in the heat of Indian summer. Before she knew it, the day came for the first literary-club meeting. Hallie was excited because Glynnis and Evie had said they'd come to hear Lowell Pippin read his newly acclaimed work, *Stargazer's Fantasies*. It was also the first meeting in the Cellar's new back room.

As Hallie set things up for the reading, she saw Joe and Daniel walk in. She missed Chino. Soon, though, she was glad he wasn't there to witness this fiasco—and her embarrassment. Lowell Pippin turned out to be a lecherous old man and his poetry bordered on the obscene. Half the membership left in a huff. Evie thought it was funny until Hallie leaned over and whispered, "The club didn't have funds to put him up in a hotel. I promised him Gram's bedroom for the night."

"Over my dead body," snarled a deep voice behind her, "or his." Hallie whipped around, shocked to see Chino threatening Lowell Pippin with bodily harm while Joe and Daniel hid discreet grins.

Chino looked so good and at the same time so fiercely protective, Hallie's heart swelled. "I didn't know you were back," she said inanely.

"You didn't get a tape for your answering machine, did you? Our negotiations in Oklahoma aren't finished, but tomorrow's the Lost Maples cook-off."

Hallie blanched. "Chino, I forgot."

"I see. So, you're backing out?"

"No. I've been busy doing lesson plans and painting classrooms. I really forgot."

"Painting?" Evie snorted. "Don't tell me. The field house won again. Hallie, come teach in San Antonio. They don't make us paint our own rooms."

Hallie retold the paint saga and was rewarded by the commiseration she'd sought weeks ago. Glynnis and Evie appreciated the irony. For a moment it felt like old times.

Pippin wound down and the three men went to deal with him. They didn't say how they resolved sleeping arrangements, and Hallie didn't ask.

"Daniel and I are going to your cook-off," Evie told Hallie after Joe and Glynnis left to catch their plane. "Chino drafted us. He's determined nothing's going to jinx you this time."

"Really?" Hallie murmured, her heart beating faster.

"Yep. I'm taking Daniel home to meet my parents tonight, and Chino's parking his motor home in your driveway. I hope you thank him."

"I can't believe I didn't remember the cook-off," Hallie lamented.

Evie put a hand on her arm. "It's not about the Cellar anymore, is it, Hallie? Why don't you call off this silly bet?"

Hallie couldn't bring herself to tell Evie she couldn't call it off because doing so might very well end all contact with Chino. Things hadn't been the same between them since San Antonio; she knew he'd been hurt by her lack of trust. She shook her head and quickly said her goodbyes, intent on avoiding further discussion.

She thought Chino would drop in for coffee. But he pulled his motor home in behind her trailer and didn't get out. After a few minutes she saw the interior lights of the vehicle wink off. She lay awake until the first rooster crowed.

Dan and Evie arrived soon after. Without further ado, they formed a caravan going down Ranch Road 187. Chino took the lead and neatly sandwiched Hallie in the middle between his rig and Daniel's van.

The first rays of sun melted the haze bracketing the lacy oaks that dotted the sloping grasslands; in spite of Chino's silence, Hallie felt a surprising sense of well-being. By the time they pulled off at the old Cider Mill for a break, her heart sang along with the upbeat tape she'd popped into her player. She would at least be near him for two whole days.

Not one of the four could resist the smell of hot apple muffins. And they washed the muffins down with the Mill's special blend of coffee. Chino bought a jug of crisp apple cider for when the day grew warm. He gave Hallie a casual hug and helped her back into her pickup. His unexpected touch stayed with her until they checked in at the park.

Once there, she realized how isolated the campsites seemed to be from one another and a sense of panic weakened her optimism. But it didn't last. Chino requested and received adjoining sites that backed onto a happily bubbling stream.

"It's early," he said. "Let's not set up yet. You said you'd never seen the maples, Hallie. To get the full effect we need to hike into Hale's Hollow. The ranger gave me a map. He said the colors up there are spectacular."

"We'll go," Daniel agreed, then shot Evie a guilty glance. "If you want to, of course."

She laughed. "After suffering through my mother's third degree last night, you deserve to make the decision."

"Ah, how was that?" Hallie murmured.

Evie grimaced. "Mother will never change. And you know, for the first time, I'm not dating someone just to please her."

Hallie thought that was a good sign and told Evie so.

The four talked as they climbed the well-shaded mountain trail. Occasionally they met other hikers coming down the trail. Other than that, they had the mountain to themselves.

At one point the two women stopped and listened to what sounded like a rippling mountain stream, trying to figure out its location.

Chino laughed. "I'm afraid you've been duped by canon wrens, ladies. They're birds that mimic rushing water. Oh, look! A golden eagle."

Arms linked, he and Hallie stood, awed by the sight.

The maples were almost anticlimactic, although as a close relative of the sugar maple, their bright autumn foliage was impressive. Hallie eyed the blaze of red, orange and yellow. "What makes them unique?" she asked.

Chino pulled out the brochure, draped an arm over her shoulder and pulled her close so they could share the information. "Apparently they're extremely rare. Especially for this climate."

"Wow," Hallie exclaimed. "It says they survived the Pleistocene ice age." She gazed at the tall trees with new respect.

Daniel shucked off his small backpack and sat on a log. "I've lived in Texas all my life. Didn't know this place existed. I'm trying to talk Evie into doing more local exploration on weekends. Are you two interested?"

Chino's hand slipped to Hallie's neck. His fingers flexed.

She glanced up and met his brooding gaze and smiled.

He seemed encouraged. "We'll discuss it," he said, bending to kiss the tip of Hallie's nose.

"Hey, no mushy stuff," Evie warned. "I vote we eat. I'm starved."

They ate the picnic lunch they'd brought and enjoyed the warmth of the sun before heading back.

The day had been so wondrous Hallie was taken aback when they arrived in camp and found Serita and Hank set up nearby.

"What are you two doing here?" Chino asked, his tone less than civil. "In all this big park, can't you find another space?"

"Why, sugar," Serita said smoothly, "one might think you're trying to keep Hallie away from other people."

Chino scowled. "What's that supposed to mean?"

Serita shot Hallie a coy smile. "Sometimes it's hard to recognize a wolf in sheep's clothing," she said before sauntering off with Hank in tow.

Hallie would've had to be blind to miss Chino's heightened color. She wondered fleetingly if it was because he couldn't abide losing Serita to Hank. She said nothing, but a pall had been cast. All evening it seemed as if Chino looked for reasons to snap at Hank. Serita acted smug enough to truly ruin Hallie's day. She and Evie slept with her ingredients that night. They rose early, half expecting to find her stove destroyed or worse. But nothing had been touched. Before long, the spicy scent of chili permeated the air.

The sun was high overhead when things began to happen—nothing Hallie could blame on anyone. First a swarm of bees took a liking to her table. She tried to shoo them away discreetly and drew Chino's attention.

He came to help, followed by Daniel who accidentally knocked down a bag of her spices. The sack split and red pepper flew everywhere. All three went into fits of sneezing.

Serita looked on. "Now I see why Babs was worried," she said.

Chino quit kicking dirt over the pile of cayenne pepper long enough to glare at her. "I take it you want one of us to ask why."

Hank curled an arm around Serita's waist. "Save your breath, babe. Delgado's got that poor girl hoodwinked."

"I'm not a girl," Hallie snapped. "And no one has me hoodwinked." Ignoring them, she opened her one spare packet of herbs and spices.

Serita shrugged. "I shouldn't even tell you what Babs said. With her own ears she heard Cody tell Ivy that Chino wanted to win so bad he'd do anything. I'm only telling you this because Chino had the nerve to suggest Hank was to blame for those pranks." She turned to leave. "I can see you don't believe me. I say it's mighty suspicious—all these bees."

Hallie dropped the spoon she was holding into her chili pot. The hot sauce splashed out and burned her arm. Tears sprang to her eyes.

Chino missed the splattering chili. He saw the tears. "She's lying, Hallie. I did suspect Hank. Still do. But I can't prove a thing."

Hallie accepted an ice cube from Evie. *Hank.* Of course. Why hadn't she thought of him before? It added up. With Serita's pipeline to Babs Delgado, those two had opportunity, as well as motive. The realization coincided with the discovery that someone had smeared honey all over the end of her table. The dirty trick made her so furious that for a moment she couldn't speak.

She glanced up and knew Chino had noticed the honey, too. She read the despair in his eyes. "I know it's not you, Chino," Hallie said quietly. "In my heart I've always known. But if Hank's the culprit—and if we can't prove it— the least we can do is make sure he doesn't win in Terlingua."

Chino didn't want to discuss Hank. He pulled Hallie into his arms and pressed a passionate kiss to her lips—a kiss of thanks and of promise.

Hank and Serita got the message. They moved across the stream, chili pots and all.

CHAPTER ELEVEN

HALLIE'S CHILI WON in Lost Maples and she supposed she should have been happier. She would have been, if Hank hadn't come in second over Chino's third. Serita gushed, promising Hank a full troupe of mariachis in Terlingua.

"Do you have performers in your corner?" Daniel asked Hallie as they repacked her pots.

"Not unless Evie and Glynnis come and sing the song they put together for last year's teacher's retirement party," she said, winking at her friend.

Evie blushed a brilliant red. "Hallie!"

"What's this?" Dan teased. "She has hidden talents?"

Hallie feigned thought. "If I recall, they were poking fun at our cafeteria food. How did that go, Evie? Something like, 'India-rubber beefsteak in insulated cheese, weenies doing flip-flops in a flood of anemic peas.' Or words to that effect."

Chino snickered. "Such potential," he murmured, jabbing Daniel with his elbow.

Dan groaned. "If they sing, Joe and I will definitely enter the margarita mix-off to drown our sorrows."

"Hey, is everyone going to this shindig?" Hallie asked.

"Wouldn't miss it for the world," Dan and Evie both replied.

Smiling, Chino hooked Hallie around the neck and buried his face in her hair. "The pressure's on. Let's both skip out."

Hallie twisted to look at him. Was he serious? "Oh, you," she scolded, on discovering him grinning from ear to ear. "After all this ruckus you'd better believe we're going after Hank. What's that battle cry again?"

Chino punched a fist in the air. "Viva Terlingua!"

"Hear, hear!" the others chorused.

"Exactly one month from today," Chino reminded them. They closed ranks and sobered, covering palms to shake hands the way sports teams do. "Hallie, you'll ride with me," he said. "It's a long drive—miles of nothing. Next week I'll be staying at the ranch, and we'll nail down all the details."

The news cheered Hallie even though she'd be at school. As they drove off she looked for Serita and Hank, but apparently they'd gone. If Hank had done all those things to discredit Chino, she couldn't bear to have him walk away with the grand prize. Suddenly another appropriate Gramism echoed in her head: *Don't find fault, Hallie. Find remedies.*

But realistically, the big cook-off took a back seat to lesson plans and grading papers. Plus, three classrooms still needed painting. Hallie had begun to feel vaguely dissatisfied with her job, a dissatisfaction that grew when Dan and Evie left. She thought a lot about the teaching job in San Antonio. What would Chino say if she applied?

Monday, not one of her literature classes went well. Hallie tried to blot out the memory later that afternoon as she carried a tray of paint to the top of the stepladder. She was stretched out full, cutting in a corner, when she heard the door open. "Go away," she growled. "Teacher's very busy."

A familiar lazy chuckle brought her head around. Paint dribbled from her brush and landed on her nose. "Chino! What are you doing here?" She swiped at the drop, but only succeeded in spreading it around.

"Well, I brought you flowers from Babs and a dinner invitation from me." He walked over to the ladder, a smile curving his lips. "I didn't expect to find you decked out in war paint. I hope it's water-based." Taking out a clean white handkerchief, he scrubbed the top of her nose.

She laughed. He had a way of banishing her black moods. Then she registered what he'd said. "Flowers from Babs? Let me guess. Poison oak, right?"

"You might say my dear sister-in-law has seen the light. We had a very illuminating conversation last night. Even Jesse butted out."

"I'd hate for you to get into a family feud on account of me, Chino." She stepped off the last rung of the ladder and set her brush aside.

"Hot-tempered as all the Delgados are, you better get used to it."

"Me?" Startled, her eyes met his over the brilliant autumn bouquet he thrust into her hands.

Chino toyed with the stiff points of her collar. "Aren't we starting over?"

She bent to sniff the blossoms. "Are we? You have a way of popping in and out of my life. Don't hurt me again, Chino."

"Oh, honey." He threaded his fingers through her silky hair and tipped her chin—forcing her to meet his somber gaze. "I've decided not to enter the Terlingua cook-off. Hank's grudge is with me. Not you."

"No. I've thought about it, too. First of all, his grudge is now with me, as well. He's trying to throw both of us—using a 'divide and conquer' strategy. Second, the Delgado tradition is at stake. And to tell you the truth, I never have found Tolbert's rules anywhere. So—" she took a deep breath "—I won't enter. You said yourself mine is a domestic recipe."

"Listen to us. That was male pride talking, Hallie. Add 'em up. Overall, your chili earned more points. Did you see Penny Beth's latest story? She quoted one judge as saying your chili has an exceptional new taste."

"Chino, I have an idea." Hallie snatched his hand, her voice rising with excitement. Tugging him across the room, she cracked open the door and glanced up and down the hall. Once she determined they were alone, she flattened herself against the door, eyes gleaming. "Let's combine forces. What if we used your recipe and my secret ingredient?''

Her proposal knocked the pins out from under him. He didn't know what to say. At last he held up a hand. "Don't do anything rash. Sleep on that proposition before you say one more word. Go put your flowers in water and hand me a brush. We're going to finish this damn paint job and then I'm taking you out for dinner. And," he drawled, "we are *not* having chili."

"Okay," she agreed, her tone equally spirited. "But I won't change my mind. My grandmother taught me that a Bergstrom's word is binding."

Chino lifted her off her feet and whirled around the front of the room. "Your grandmother was quite a lady."

"She was," Hallie said breathlessly as he set her down. "Mostly, she was wise and practical. Yet at times she was funny. And passionate when she really believed in something."

"Then she'd be pleased to know you're very like her." Chino's observation was rough with feeling.

Hallie touched his cheek, too moved to speak. In a hailstorm of emotions, she hurried to find a vase. When she returned with a paint roller for Chino, talk turned to less personal matters. They reminisced about experiences in the old school; Chino's memories were certainly more adventurous and funnier than Hallie's.

An hour later, the painting was completed, and Hallie found herself seated across from Chino in a candlelit restaurant. A place she'd never before considered going dressed as she was. That was something else she loved about Chino—his easy self-assurance.

This dinner launched a courtship the likes of which Hallie had only dared explore in the privacy of her dreams. Beginning the next day, Chino took her to school in the mornings and picked her up every night. They laughed together, played together and often dined together.

They did not, however, sleep together.

Two weeks went by before Hallie came out of the clouds long enough to admit that if he asked, she would probably roll out a red carpet to her bed.

Another week faded before it dawned on her—Chino hadn't broached the subject of uniting their recipes, never mind their lives.

With the big cook-off only seven days away, Hallie simply took matters into her own hands. "We're going to my house to make chili tonight," she informed Chino. "Combined. Your recipe . . . my lingonberries."

He twined their hands and tugged her across the seat for a kiss. "Are those anything like farkleberries?" he teased.

"No, silly. Gram ordered the bushes from Denmark. They're a Scandinavian delicacy. Kind of a cross between a cranberry and a blueberry, but smaller. Very red in color. Quite sweet, yet a little tart."

He looked shocked. "You aren't kidding."

Extremely self-satisfied, she smiled and shook her head.

"I'll be damned," he marveled on the drive across town. "I never would have guessed. And, Hallie, I didn't expect you to share your trade secret."

He had pulled into her driveway before she answered. "Gram used to say real love begins when nothing's expected in return." She lifted her chin and looked him in the eye. "I never understood what she meant—until now. It's my gift to you, Chino. No strings attached."

The significance of her words landed like a well-aimed punch to his midsection. She'd as much as said she loved him. Chino didn't know how to respond. His heart swelled, then shattered into a zillion falling pieces. A kiss seemed inadequate. But it was all he could muster, considering she had once again floored him with her generosity.

Hallie tasted a change in Chino's kiss. There was love and a humbleness that gave her the power to hurt him as he'd hurt her those many years ago—whether he'd meant to or not. A power she swore here and now never to use. Love came with responsibilities and risks, she realized, fully understanding why he'd run. They'd been too young, too vulnerable, for risks.

He drew back and stroked her face. "Will you trust me to make all the arrangements for Terlingua? If Hank was to try anything..."

A knot relaxed in her stomach. He was talking about her safety. Somehow, at the very least, she'd expected to be whisked off to bed.

"Absolutely," she said, smiling. "My secret ingredient and my life are in your hands."

But by midweek, she began to rue giving him carte blanche with either. At night her kitchen became a chili test site. Her living room, a beehive of activity for the Delgado women, who hauled in bolts of calico and silk and patterns of period costumes they said were absolutely essential to the Terlingua event. The Delgado men were slated to wear brocade vests, string ties and sleeve garters reminiscent of the Old West. In keeping with the theme, Ivy insisted the women have long dresses with sweetheart necklines and leg-of-mutton sleeves.

At the first fitting, Hallie protested. Her dress was lovely—slender and elegant in palest cream silk. "It's a ghost town," she complained, "smack in the middle of the Chihuahua Desert. Dirt. Cholla. Dirt. Creosote bushes. More dirt. The dress'll be ruined."

Ivy shrugged. "Too late. It's already cut to your size."

Hallie twisted in front of the full-length mirror and sighed. With her hair pulled loosely atop her head the way Louisa arranged it, she resembled a pioneer bride. She felt a tiny fissure of longing, but thrust it aside, accepting that their courtship was on hold until Chino beat Hank Edwards once and for all.

Meanwhile, Gram's kitchen was a hotbed of activity. They mixed, they tasted, dumped and mixed again until the night before the cook-off, when everyone, including Ram who'd been hard to please, pronounced they had a winner.

It pained Hallie to watch Chino blend her beautiful red lingonberries into a paste with his smelly horseradish, but she had to admit the result tingled her palate and pleased her tastebuds. That night, the two of them stayed behind to carefully measure out the exact ingredients.

When they were finished, Chino kissed her and said, "Come, Hallie, I want you at the ranch tonight, where I'll know you're safe."

The guest room was serenely attractive, but Hallie was so keyed up, she hardly slept a wink.

"You're awfully quiet," Chino said to her the next day as they pulled into Fort Stockton to gas up the motor home. "Having second thoughts about not entering yourself?"

She grasped his hand, her palm damp. "Second thoughts for you. I love you, Chino, and Hank Edwards strikes me as a sore loser."

"You pick the damnedest time to tell a guy you love him. There must be twenty rigs lined up behind me. Don't worry about me—you just hold that first thought. Hear?"

Hallie laughed. And as they left, the sun rising jaggedly over the Chisos Mountains bathed her in happiness and banished all her fears.

In a way, Terlingua reminded Hallie of Buzzard Flats. In springtime, it might be pretty, with ocotillo and prairie verbena in bloom. In November, everything was the color of the adobe compound, except for the cliffs streaked with cinnabar deposits; they were left over from the mines that had once made the place a boomtown.

Hallie soon discovered it was the people, the ones who came from all over the world every year to boast about their chili prowess, that lent charm to this granddaddy of all cook-offs. People who were probably normal in any other setting dressed up and acted weird in the name of chili.

When Evie, Dan, Glynnis and Joe arrived looking like bushrangers, Hallie shook her head in amusement. A moment later she spied Hank and Serita and no longer felt amused. But she was soon happily distracted by the arrival of Ram and Martha, who greeted her with fond exuberance.

Beer flowed freely; tequila, too, in the form of frosty margaritas. But no one was going anywhere that night; no one was driving, so it was hard not to join in. Especially when some group was always selling tickets for chances on a booze wagon—a child's wagon heaped high with all manner of spirits.

It seemed to Hallie that everyone knew and liked the Delgado men. Chino kept an arm around her waist, refusing to let her hide when the rest of them introduced the women in their lives. "Chino," she chided, at one point, "that man you called the Judge thinks we're engaged!"

"Really?" Chino tipped his Stetson forward and took another swig from his long-necked beer.

Hallie peeked over his shoulder and eyed the fellow who was walking away. He sported a snowy Santa Claus mane. "Is he really a judge?"

"Yep," Ram answered. "Hangin' or marryin'. Say, it's gettin' kind of warm out here, darlin'. Let's go inside where I can beat you at chess."

"Ha!" Hallie said, but she let herself be drawn in. Not long after they'd set up the board, she heard laughter and loud thunks outside the window. She got up to look. Chino, his brothers and a bunch of other men were pitching metal washers into a can sunk in the ground. She liked watching him having a good time. She liked watching him, period.

Three times she beat Ram before he gave up. Then Chino popped in to see if she was ready to meet some of the people entered in the black-eyed-pea and bean contests. "Lead on," she instructed. "Your dad's going to sulk for a while. He doesn't like losing, you know."

In the waning sunlight, smoke rolled from some of the most elaborate cookers Hallie had ever seen. With Chino at her side, their arms loosely linked, she bought souvenirs, sampled long curls of Texas fries and in general immersed herself in nostalgia. All in all, she was content.

Her lassitude continued into the next morning, when she donned her old-fashioned dress. Louisa offered to do her hair. Ivy insisted on weaving cornflowers among the tresses.

Babs looked her over critically and, surprisingly congenial, added a necklace—a lacy cameo on a blue velvet band that she said had belonged to Chino's mother.

"But... but I couldn't." Hallie's objection that something could happen to it was of no avail. The Delgado women were as stubborn as their men.

Outside, Daniel and Joe hovered over Chino's sizzling chili. As overseer, Chino was resplendent in black hat, black pants, white ruffled shirt and black string tie. Hallie's heart turned over just watching him.

"Show time," Ivy murmured as a vehicle they'd dubbed the horseless carriage rumbled to a stop. Ram was driving and Martha sat beside him, elegant in a picture hat. The rest of the women made quite a sight in their colorful dresses. Everyone piled into the rickety, open-topped rig, which had a set of real long-horned cattle horns tied to its front grill.

Crushed against Chino, Hallie felt the mood shift. Before she could analyze why, Ram took off in a swirl of dust, causing her heart to slam against her breastbone. "What's happening?" she whispered.

Chino smiled, then kissed her softly as Ram stopped near the stage.

"Oh, no," Hallie sputtered. "We are *not* going to sing." She had just spied Evie and Glynnis on stage wildly gesturing to the Judge.

The good-size crowd quieted and watched the proceedings.

"I won't be tricked into doing some stupid song," Hallie insisted as Chino dragged her from the vehicle. The Judge had the microphone. He drowned her protest, talking about wedding ceremonies he performed here every year. "Folks, if there are objections to Chino Delgado and Hallie Bergstrom being joined in holy wedlock, you better speak up now or forever hold your peace."

Hallie skidded to a halt. She gaped at Chino's grinning family. Her mouth went dry and she looked at Chino, her eyes begging him to stop this farce. But he was fumbling in his pockets, and Jesse was helping, looking very stern.

Ram took Hallie's arm. Still, she hung back. "Why me? I never said I'd be part of any entertainment."

"Who gives this woman?" the Judge demanded in a thunderous voice.

"May I?" Ram asked, pulling Hallie close. "In the absence of your grandmother, it'd purely pleasure me, darlin'."

Suddenly Hallie found herself standing on stage beside Chino in front of the Judge. Chino's voice was strong as he repeated the vows. Her voice tripped over every word. The band of diamonds he slid onto her finger winked in the sunlight. Hallie panicked. "I...I don't have one for y-you."

Glynnis stepped up and pressed a matching band into her cold hand. Hallie almost dropped it. "This looks real," she breathed. Chino had to help her slip it onto his finger while the Judge pronounced them husband and wife. Then Chino gathered her into his arms for an all-consuming kiss. The crowd went wild, cheering and clapping.

"It's just an act," Hallie insisted when strangers pressed in from all sides and offered good wishes.

Chino shared a firm handshake with Dutch and accepted a resounding smack on the lips and congratulations from Mama Claire.

"You said you trusted me to set things up," he reminded Hallie, dropping a kiss on her nose.

"Yes, but—"

"You gave me your secret ingredient with no strings attached."

"Yes, but—"

"Your secret ingredient, you said—and your life."

"Yes, I did. But—"

"Well, all I have to give you is my name and a lifetime of love. Will you accept that?"

Jesse Delgado swept her into a bear hug before she could reply. "Gotta keep all this chili talent together," he exclaimed, setting Hallie down. Clapping Chino on the back, he moved on.

"Is that what this is about?" Hallie asked Chino in a low voice. "Chili? Are we proving something—like maybe to Hank and Serita?"

Guitars from an impromptu jam session began to throb in the background. "They've gone," he said. "Word of what he's done passed through the ranks last night. Hank admitted everything. He's no longer welcome to cook anywhere with this group. I told you Texans take chili seriously."

Martha slipped away from Ram and gave Hallie a kiss on the cheek. "You've made Ram very happy," she said. "He was really worried about which of you to support down here. I didn't want him to even come." She caught Chino's hand and beamed. "Now when that chili wins, you both win."

"So it is true?" Hallie rose on tiptoe and kissed Chino. "We're really married? And you're not just doing this out of gratitude?"

"Yes, ma'am. No, ma'am," he drawled, kissing her back. "I have no altruistic motives. If we didn't have to go cook chili, I'd show you, too."

She dared not picture what he meant. Not yet, at any rate.

Their wedding kicked off a frenzy of activity that continued throughout the day. Groups hawking the chili of various teams with crazy names performed at regular intervals, vying for the best show. Bachelorettes chased Mr. Terlingua, who'd been voted in the night before. He, in turn, openly lusted after Miss Terlingua, a leggy brunette with green eyes.

About midday, *Don't Mess with Texas* flags snapped to attention in the stiff breeze that blew in from the south across the shadowy Mesa de Anguila.

Chino and Hallie blocked out everything and everyone but their chili and each other. "How about a Christmas honeymoon?" he asked unexpectedly, as she dumped their secret mixture into the thick chili. "A Caribbean cruise."

She stopped stirring. "Oh, Chino. Where will we live?"

"San Antonio or Cedarville. It's your choice, Hallie."

"I love your home, but I could never part with Gram's."

"Don't. We'll keep both. Besides, we owe her, don't you think?"

Hallie nodded and smiled through sudden tears. Before she could thank him, it was time for the judging. Together they filled the cup. With friends and relatives gathered around, they made the long walk to the judging tables.

Hallie soon discovered that judging chili for the best of the best was no speedy matter. Each entry passed through three sets of very serious judges. As judges tasted and marked their sheets, she alternately chewed her fingernails and dug them into Chino's arm. "Relax," he said for about the hundredth time. "If we win, fine. If not..." He said no more.

"You'll win," Jesse assured them. "Then our sons will carry on the chili tradition."

Chino met Hallie's eyes, touched his mother's cameo where it rested in the hollow of her throat and growled his assent. She felt the tips of her ears heat over what Jesse's statement implied. And from that moment on, they were both impatient with a judging process that seemed to take forever.

By the time third place was announced and their number hadn't yet been called, Chino was ready to pack it in. "It doesn't matter," he said. "We have each other."

Hallie insisted they wait it out.

Finally, only first place was left. Their number was read out, and she hugged Chino around the neck so hard he found it impossible to climb onto the stage. He all but carried her along, insisting she accept the special championship flag while he collected the plaque and a huge silver belt buckle.

"Hey, Delgado," someone yelled. "What's the secret of this win?"

"Lingonberries," he shouted, winking at Hallie.

"Sure! Tell us another one," the disgruntled loser called back. "With you being in the business, I expected the truth, at least."

And on that note they left.

They laughed all the way home. Somewhere on the long drive, both agreed that Terlingua would live in their hearts forever. Not only had a marriage been forged and tradition served, but Gram's lingonberries would go down in the annals of chili history as yet another whopping Texas chili spoof.

Later, following a more private ceremony in the family church, Hallie and Chino shared love in the fullest sense. Lying nestled in one another's arms in the old four-poster that had been Gram's, Hallie sensed her grandmother's approval.

Sated by love and on the verge of sleep, she would never know for certain if she dreamed it or if the feisty old woman transcended time to whisper, "Viva Terlingua, child."

Hallie and Chino's Winning Chili Recipe

4 lbs trimmed sirloin, cubed
4 tbsp olive oil
1 shot tequila
1 quart water
1 jalapeño pepper, finely chopped
1 large onion, chopped
1 clove garlic, minced
1 tsp ginger
1 tsp cumin
1 tsp coriander
dash of salt and black pepper
Chino's Secret Ingredient—2 tbsp horseradish
Hallie and Gram's Secret Ingredient—¾ cup ground lingonberries

Using a large, heavy pan, braise meat in olive oil with onion and garlic. Add water. Mix remaining ingredients, except secret ingredients, and add to pan.

Cook slowly, covered, for 4 to 5 hours. One-half hour before serving, uncover and add secret ingredients. Stir well and simmer.

Serve over cornbread or rice.

Author's Note: Cook-off chili is an acquired taste!

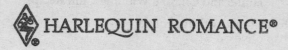

HARLEQUIN ROMANCE®

brings you

Harlequin Romance wishes you a *Merry Christmas...*
with two special Kids & Kisses stories!

In December, watch for *The Santa Sleuth*
by Heather Allison and *The Nutcracker Prince*
by Rebecca Winters.

Romances that celebrate love, families, children—
and Christmas!

The Santa Sleuth by Heather Allison
Virginia McEnery, age six, is the official "Santa sleuth"
on one of Houston's TV newscasts. Her job is to research
shopping mall Santas. And she whispers her Christmas
wish to every one of them. *A mommy.* Even though her
dad, Kirk, doesn't know it yet, she's already made her
choice—TV news producer Amanda Donnelly.

The Nutcracker Prince by Rebecca Winters
Anna Roberts, age six, wants a *daddy* for Christmas. Her
own daddy. Anna's sure he looks just like the handsome
Nutcracker Prince in her mommy's beautiful book. And
she's right! Because shortly before Christmas, her daddy
appears. His name is Konstantin and he's come here from
Russia. And he wants to marry Meg, her mom....

Available wherever Harlequin books are sold. KIDS7

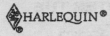 HARLEQUIN ® 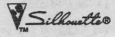 Silhouette®

The movie event of the season can be the reading event of the year!

Lights... The lights go on in October when CBS presents Harlequin/Silhouette Sunday Matinee Movies. These four movies are based on bestselling Harlequin and Silhouette novels.

Camera... As the cameras roll, be the first to read the original novels the movies are based on!

Action... Through this offer, you can have these books sent directly to you! Just fill in the order form below and you could be reading the books...before the movie!

48288-4	Treacherous Beauties by Cheryl Emerson		
	$3.99 U.S./$4.50 CAN.		☐
83305-9	Fantasy Man by Sharon Green		
	$3.99 U.S./$4.50 CAN.		☐
48289-2	A Change of Place by Tracy Sinclair		
	$3.99 U.S./$4.50CAN.		☐
83306-7	Another Woman by Margot Dalton		
	$3.99 U.S./$4.50 CAN.		☐

TOTAL AMOUNT $ _____
POSTAGE & HANDLING $ _____
($1.00 for one book, 50¢ for each additional)
APPLICABLE TAXES* $ _____
<u>**TOTAL PAYABLE**</u> $ _____
(check or money order—please do not send cash)

To order, complete this form and send it, along with a check or money order for the total above, payable to Harlequin Books, to: **In the U.S.:** 3010 Walden Avenue, P.O. Box 9047, Buffalo, NY 14269-9047; **In Canada:** P.O. Box 613, Fort Erie, Ontario, L2A 5X3.

Name: _____

Address: _____ City: _____

State/Prov.: _____ Zip/Postal Code: _____

*New York residents remit applicable sales taxes.
  Canadian residents remit applicable GST and provincial taxes.   CBSPR

IT'S FREE! IT'S FUN! ENTER THE

☆ "Hooray for Hollywood" ☆

SWEEPSTAKES!

We're giving away prizes to celebrate the screening of four new romance movies on CBS TV this fall! Look for the movies on four Sunday afternoons in October. And be sure to return your Official Entry Coupons to try for a fabulous **vacation in Hollywood!**

 If you're the Grand Prize winner we'll fly you and your companion to Los Angeles for a 7-day/6-night vacation you'll never forget!

 You'll stay at the luxurious Regent Beverly Wilshire Hotel,* a prime location for celebrity spotting!

 You'll have time to visit Universal Studios,* stroll the Hollywood Walk of Fame, check out celebrities' footprints at Mann's Chinese Theater, ride a trolley to see the homes of the stars, and more!

 The prize includes a rental car for 7 days and $1,000.00 pocket money!

Someone's going to win this fabulous prize, and it might just be you! Remember, the more times you enter, the better your chances of winning!

---

* Five hundred entrants will each receive **SUNGLASSES OF THE STARS!** Don't miss out. **ENTER TODAY!**

The proprietors of the trademark are not associated with this promotion.

CBS!BC

"HOORAY FOR HOLLYWOOD" SWEEPSTAKES

HERE'S HOW THE SWEEPSTAKES WORKS

OFFICIAL RULES — NO PURCHASE NECESSARY

To enter, complete an Official Entry Form or hand print on a 3" x 5" card the words "HOORAY FOR HOLLYWOOD", your name and address and mail your entry in the pre-addressed envelope (if provided) or to: "Hooray for Hollywood" Sweepstakes, P.O. Box 9076, Buffalo, NY 14269-9076 or "Hooray for Hollywood" Sweepstakes, P.O. Box 637, Fort Erie, Ontario L2A 5X3. Entries must be sent via First Class Mail and be received no later than 12/31/94. No liability is assumed for lost, late or misdirected mail.

Winners will be selected in random drawings to be conducted no later than January 31, 1995 from all eligible entries received.

Grand Prize: A 7-day/6-night trip for 2 to Los Angeles, CA including round trip air transportation from commercial airport nearest winner's residence, accommodations at the Regent Beverly Wilshire Hotel, free rental car, and $1,000 spending money. (Approximate prize value which will vary dependent upon winner's residence: $5,400.00 U.S.); 500 Second Prizes: A pair of "Hollywood Star" sunglasses (prize value: $9.95 U.S. each). Winner selection is under the supervision of D.L. Blair, Inc., an independent judging organization, whose decisions are final. Grand Prize travelers must sign and return a release of liability prior to traveling. Trip must be taken by 2/1/96 and is subject to airline schedules and accommodations availability.

Sweepstakes offer is open to residents of the U.S. (except Puerto Rico) and Canada who are 18 years of age or older, except employees and immediate family members of Harlequin Enterprises, Ltd., its affiliates, subsidiaries, and all agencies, entities or persons connected with the use, marketing or conduct of this sweepstakes. All federal, state, provincial, municipal and local laws apply. Offer void wherever prohibited by law. Taxes and/or duties are the sole responsibility of the winners. Any litigation within the province of Quebec respecting the conduct and awarding of prizes may be submitted to the Regie des loteries et courses du Quebec. All prizes will be awarded; winners will be notified by mail. No substitution of prizes are permitted. Odds of winning are dependent upon the number of eligible entries received.

Potential grand prize winner must sign and return an Affidavit of Eligibility within 30 days of notification. In the event of non-compliance within this time period, prize may be awarded to an alternate winner. Prize notification returned as undeliverable may result in the awarding of prize to an alternate winner. By acceptance of their prize, winners consent to use of their names, photographs, or likenesses for purpose of advertising, trade and promotion on behalf of Harlequin Enterprises, Ltd., without further compensation unless prohibited by law. A Canadian winner must correctly answer an arithmetical skill-testing question in order to be awarded the prize.

For a list of winners (available after 2/28/95), send a separate stamped, self-addressed envelope to: Hooray for Hollywood Sweepstakes 3252 Winners, P.O. Box 4200, Blair, NE 68009.

CBSRLS

OFFICIAL ENTRY COUPON

"Hooray for Hollywood"
SWEEPSTAKES!

Yes, I'd love to win the Grand Prize — a vacation in Hollywood — or one of 500 pairs of "sunglasses of the stars"! Please enter me in the sweepstakes!

This entry must be received by December 31, 1994.
Winners will be notified by January 31, 1995.

Name _____

Address _____ Apt. _____

City _____

State/Prov. _____ Zip/Postal Code _____

Daytime phone number _____
(area code)

Mail all entries to: Hooray for Hollywood Sweepstakes,
P.O. Box 9076, Buffalo, NY 14269-9076.
In Canada, mail to: Hooray for Hollywood Sweepstakes,
P.O. Box 637, Fort Erie, ON L2A 5X3.

KCH

OFFICIAL ENTRY COUPON

"Hooray for Hollywood"
SWEEPSTAKES!

Yes, I'd love to win the Grand Prize — a vacation in Hollywood — or one of 500 pairs of "sunglasses of the stars"! Please enter me in the sweepstakes!

This entry must be received by December 31, 1994.
Winners will be notified by January 31, 1995.

Name _____

Address _____ Apt. _____

City _____

State/Prov. _____ Zip/Postal Code _____

Daytime phone number _____
(area code)

Mail all entries to: Hooray for Hollywood Sweepstakes,
P.O. Box 9076, Buffalo, NY 14269-9076.
In Canada, mail to: Hooray for Hollywood Sweepstakes,
P.O. Box 637, Fort Erie, ON L2A 5X3.

KCH